Roberta Samuels

LOST

An Ancient Artifact Adrift in Sarasota Bay

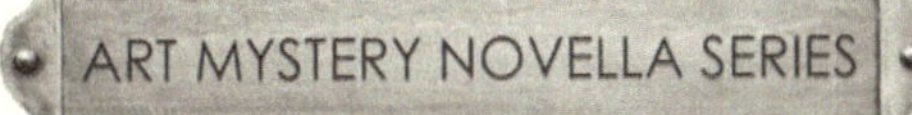

Published by Red Penguin Books

Bellerose Village, New York

ISBN

Print 978-1-63777-752-7 | 978-1-63777-753- 4

Digital 978-1-63777-751-0

Roberta Samuels

LOST

An Ancient Artifact Adrift in Sarasota Bay

ART MYSTERY NOVELLA SERIES

For Nate, with love and esteem

CHAPTER ONE

I turned the key in the lock, and the front door of my little Spanish-style house swung quietly open. It felt good to be home. My boyfriend, Sam, was right behind me as we stepped directly into the living room.

My name is Barbara Waldheim, and Sam and I had just returned from spending three months at our summer house in the little French village of Montpezat de Quercy. We loved it there but were happy to be back in Sarasota for the winter before returning to France for another summer next year. Sam and I were one of those happy couples who had found one another after failed relationships with other people. We had been together for five years now, dividing our time between Sarasota in the winter and my 15th-century townhouse in a village in southwest France in the summer.

We looked around the space we remembered so well and so

fondly. It took a moment for our eyes to adjust to the muted light after the bright sunshine outside. "Oh, my God! What happened here?" My eyes focused on the sisal carpet in front of the fireplace. "What happened to the new rug? It's ruined! It's all deformed—not to mention, filthy."

"Looks like something was chewing on it," Sam said, bending down to examine the misshapen thing. "There seems to be a lot of dog hair on it."

"Dog hair? Waylan told me he didn't have a dog! 'No pets allowed' was our rental agreement." The minute I said it, I became aware of a distinctive doggy odor hanging over everything.

"Well, it looks like Waylan wasn't a very good listener," Sam said in his usual understated manner. Sam kept his cool, while I, meanwhile, was livid. He pointed to an empty pack of Marlboro's on the leather sofa. "No smoking either?"

"Damn Waylan. He was such a sweet talker. He told me exactly what I wanted to hear." My shoulders sagged. It had been a long trek home, and we deserved a nicer homecoming than this.

"We'd better check around for any other damage." Sam moved away and began looking around the big, open living area.

"Where's the lamp?" I wondered as we moved out into the hall toward the spare bedroom. We soon found the 'other damage' by the French doors of the side entrance. "Look at all this broken glass." I was aghast. "Have we been burgled, too?"

Sam let out a low whistle. "I wonder what went on here. Looks like your renter forgot his key and broke the door glass to get inside. He tried to clean up, but what a hopeless effort."

"The vacuum cleaner!" It was my pride and joy. Weird, I know, but it cost a fortune and was a wonderful machine. The best vacuum cleaner I've ever owned. I flew to the closet where it was kept and dragged it out to check it over. It was full of glass shards. Destroyed, in fact. I could have cried. "He's ruined it. What idiot vacuums up glass?!" I wailed.

"The one you rented to. Why did you ever lease your house to that lowlife, Barbara? Why did you rent at all for the short period we were gone?" Sam asked for the tenth time, and for the tenth time, I felt like the world's biggest fool.

"I've told you. I thought that I could make a little money while we were away. I interviewed Waylan, and he told me how much he loved my place and what good care he would take of it. He turned on the 'good ole boy' southern charm, and I fell for it. He had me bamboozled."

It was a pretty lame excuse, and I knew it. Out of all the prospective renters, Waylan had been the cutest, and I was flustered and in a hurry to get packed and going. Everything seemed fine.

The house belonged to me after my divorce. Sam owned a condo on a lake in a golfing community, and we divided our time between the two places as seemed convenient or desirable to us.

Sam snorted. "I wish you'd consulted me. You sure were taken in." Sam would never have been taken in by Waylan's sexy smile—unlike me. I felt miserable. "And if you think that he was ever going to leave at the end of the lease period, you were sadly mistaken," he continued. "It was going to take a bomb under him to get a guy like that outta here. And talk about paying you rent—you musta been dreaming." Sam was getting worked up. A rare event. I was already worked up. This was another instance where we were in total agreement. As soon as it became apparent Waylan Cooper was not honoring his side of the bargain and paying his rent in a timely fashion, I lowered the boom.

"Waylan was planning to stiff you," he said. "The old slow-pay scam, and you would have been screwed trying to do anything about it. Have you any idea of the heap of trouble you'd be in trying to evict him and reclaim your own property! You'd be out a fortune—"

"Okay, Sam. Okay. For the *umpteenth* time, I was stupid to get involved with him. I was a patsy. I just wanted to make a little extra income for our holiday in France. Luckily, you saw the way things were going and put me on guard against him." But almost too late. Sam had learned all about my renting woes once he'd landed in Toulouse for our summer together. I was retired and free to precede him to France, while he had to wait for his vacation since he was still working.

"I don't mean to restate the obvious. I was only watching out for you." Sam relented, a little embarrassed. "The best piece of luck was that Jack and Jill knew exactly how to deal with him. They know the score with sleazeballs like Waylan Cooper."

He was right. Jack and Jill Gilbert are old friends of ours who happen to be private investigators, among many things. It took a lot of side hustles to float their boat, but they always seemed to squeak by. As they said themselves, they were the original Jack and Jill, always trying to make it up that hill.

"Yeah," I said, glad to focus on the happy outcome of my entanglement with a less-than-desirable renter. "And give me some credit, why don't you? I didn't waste a minute, did I? As soon as he didn't pay rent, I called them for advice and they told me what to do. Based on your tip-off, I took action." It was very satisfying to imagine Waylan opening the door to an official notice that his lease period was up. "Waylan didn't know what hit him."

We continued our tour of the house, walking back through the hall into the living room. Dusk was beginning to fall, and the light in the room was growing dim. "Where *is* my lamp?" I wondered aloud again, looking around, in case he'd shoved it away in a corner or something.

"What's this weird thing?" Sam asked, pointing to a stone carving with a broken corner on the mantelpiece. It was an ugly, dull color, rough and covered with dense symbols, incised into the surface.

"That's not mine," I said, as my eye swept disapprovingly over the ash left in the fireplace. It was dusty everywhere. "It looks like a tourist souvenir or something. Like someone's idea of the tablets of the Ten Commandments. This room hasn't been dusted since I left!"

Sam hefted the carving in his hands. "It's not too heavy. I kind of like it," he said. "It looks Middle Eastern."

"Waylan was a veteran. Maybe he served in the Middle East somewhere and brought it back," I said absentmindedly, heading for the kitchen, more concerned with that than Waylan's stupid souvenir.

Nothing in the kitchen seemed too disastrous, at first. Dirty, yes, but not damaged. It looked like Waylan wasn't much of a cook and either ate out or ordered in, judging by the cartons overflowing from the trash can. The inside of the microwave looked like an explosion in a sauce can. "I might just buy a new one," I muttered, shutting the door and moving on to the den.

The TV room or den looked okay, though it stank of stale cigarettes, and the couch had a coating of dog hair. I found several empty beer cans tossed behind it. "I'll need to hire a professional cleaning service," I said as we moved on to the master bedroom. I was dreading this room the most. If it were a mess, then I'd be staying at Sam's place this evening. No way was I sleeping in a room full of dog hair. I was allergic, and I'd be wheezing all night.

It looked all right at first glance. What a relief!

"Is this yours, my sweet?" Sam held up a lacy thong lying halfway under the bed.

"Yuck," was all I could muster.

He stifled a laugh. "I think you need to reclaim your space, my love. Meanwhile, let's grab your suitcases, and you can stay at my place tonight. Or at least until we get this place sanitized."

"Great idea." I felt my shoulders relax. Tomorrow I would awaken invigorated and more able to deal with this wreck. I'd call around for house cleaning services and put a few things out on the curb for garbage removal day, like my vacuum cleaner, microwave, and sisal rug. Then I'd have to work on replacing them.

Who knew what state the bed linen and bath towels were in? I'd check them out in the morning. No matter what, it was all going to cost a pretty penny, and none of it would be coming from Mr. Cooper.

Aside from the breakage and mess and the cost, Waylan had left a massive sense of disappointment behind him.

CHAPTER TWO

"PRIVATE EYES ARE WATCHING YOU"
~ Hall & Oates

The following day started with a whirlwind of phone calls and putting things in order at my house. Luckily, Sam had a few days off before starting back to work at the hydraulic valve plant and was happy to help before heading to the gym and then to buy groceries.

To take a break, I was heading over to Jack and Jill Gilbert's to catch up on our respective summers and to give them a huge "thank you" for their advice on how to handle Waylan Cooper's attempted house takeover. They had saved me a ton of trouble, and boy, was I ever grateful.

I liked visiting their house off of Bee Ridge Road. It sat on a winding street of cookie-cutter, ranch-style houses, which had become differentiated over the years by paint colors and the addition of lanais, pool cages, and second-story additions. Jack and Jill's house was surrounded by a big lawn, as it was set on a corner lot. As usual, I spotted a snowy egret, or Interstate 80 bird (because there are so many of them to be found on I-80), standing on their asphalt shingle roof near the pool cage. I parked at the curb, followed the little walk to the front door, and rang the bell. It had hardly finished its chime before the door swung open and my old friend Jill pulled me inside. I gave her a hug and then snuck up on Jack, who was at his usual place in the office in front of the computer screen.

"Hey there, gorgeous." He laughed as I tapped him on the left shoulder, and he turned that way while I was waiting for him on his right. I gave him a quick squeeze. If he stood up, Jack would tower over me, but sitting down, I could get to him. Jack had sandy hair, which was beginning to thin, and watery blue eyes. Jill was always complaining that he spent too much time on the computer, and it was damaging his eyesight, but he denied it. "You're making a fuss over nothing. My eyes are fine." He was in decent shape and a fast talker, betraying his New York origins, but he loved Florida, even though he always said it was Jill who'd dragged him down here. Jill was from the Panhandle, which was in the northwest part of the state toward Georgia, with its Air Force bases and not much else. Sarasota was the big city by comparison.

"Come on, I made some iced tea," Jill said. "He'll join us later; he's in the middle of something right now."

"I'll let you work," I said, and left Jack to follow Jill to the kitchen. Jill was a pretty, middle-aged woman like me, bigger boned and a bit more careworn.

My friends were obviously in one of their truce periods when they got along quite well. They ran a small tile business whose specialty was restoring Mexican tile. That's how we met, when they helped me redo my kitchen flooring. But their real passion was their second business as private investigators. They mostly did surveillance on cheating spouses or worked for insurance companies, checking that injured claimants didn't get up and go dancing when they thought nobody was looking. My friends were both licensed to carry a pistol.

Jill and Jack were much like their eponymous nursery rhyme, always trailing up the hill, always tumbling down again, and always together through it all. Yes, they were usually behind on their mortgage payments, and yes, they were often on the verge of splitting up, but somehow, they always hung on to the house, their businesses, and one another.

Whenever I visited them, it was kind of like old home week because their house was furnished with a lot of my old things. Cast off furniture and lamps that I didn't want or need anymore had been put to good use at their home. Jill honored me by having a few of my paintings hanging on her walls. I was an artist, and she had actually salvaged them from the dumpster where I had thrown them out in a fit of depression right after my divorce. Boy, but we had some history together.

Jill sat me down on my former sofa and put an iced tea in my hand. "So, how was the house when you got back?" Her eyes said it all. She knew exactly the kind of tenant Waylan was.

"You'll never believe what he did to my vacuum cleaner!" I complained. It took ten whole minutes of me venting until she finally took me in hand. "Barbara!"

"He destroyed my new rug."

"Barbara…"

"I mean, deformed it! And my Van Briggle lamp? Nowhere to be found, for God's sake."

"Barbara," she said more firmly. "If you want to recover for the damage Waylan did, you should file an action in small claims court."

"Really? You mean I could make him pay for the vacuum

and the rug?" I smiled at the thought. "And the microwave and the lamp. And the rent I'm due." My smile got broader.

"Yes." Jill nodded. "You can recover up to $1,500 in damages without a lawyer. You just go down to the Sarasota courthouse and fill out the paperwork."

"What happens then?"

Jack chimed in from the office. "The court will set a date for Waylan to appear to answer your charges."

"I'll have to confront him in person?" I hesitated. That might be an ordeal.

"Yes, you will," Jack said.

"If he shows up," Jill added. "If he doesn't appear, the court will hold him in contempt. You won't get any money, but you will have put others on notice that he's a bad risk."

"That seems worth doing. Just to warn other people, at the very least. I'd like Waylan to face some consequences for the way he treated me. Thanks, guys. I think I'll do it."

"And Barbara, maybe you should take out a restraining order against him. He isn't going to be any better disposed toward you than he is already when he gets this court order.And that guy has a shotgun." Jack's words were like a bucket of cold water.

Jill nodded. "I saw it lying on the floor of his truck one day when we were watching him."

"A gun! I don't want to rile a guy with a gun," I whined.

"All in a day's work," said Jack. "They're the ones usually needing riling."

"Now, honey," Jill said, "go easy on Barbara. She had a bad experience."

"I'm gonna think about it." I decided.

"Ask Sam," Jack said. "He'll give you good advice."

Sure, he would. Sam usually liked to let sleeping dogs lie, though.

"What are you working on at the computer, Jack?" I asked. "Anything interesting?"

Jack called me over and told me that he was on to something big. He showed me a long list of telephone numbers on the screen. His eyes shone with excitement as he explained that he was on the trail of terrorists or terrorist funding. He explained that he was working for ICE now, or at least he hoped to be working for them soon. ICE was the United States Immigration and Customs Enforcement. I was impressed.

He had hired some new workers recently for the tile company. Their papers said they were Yemeni. He noticed that these guys, who basically earned minimum wage, had fancy cars. Very fancy cars. One week, it was a Mercedes; the next week, the same guy had a Lexus. The same sort of thing for his friends.

This tight-knit group lived together in a small rental. Jack knew this because he sometimes picked them up for work in his truck. They spent a lot of time on their cell phones when they weren't pushing brooms or sponging the grout off newly laid tile. These workers seemed too well-educated to be doing the scut work he was paying them for. So, Jack got suspicious.

"Don't forget, Barbara, Sarasota was where Mohamed Atta and the other terrorist bombers spent time before 9/11. They lived in Prestancia, that gated community not far from here. They learned how to fly at that little flight school over in Venice." His words reminded me of that terrible time when the Twin Towers were bombed and the awful realization of the part Sarasota played in it.

Jill said, "I heard that they were never very good at landings, but whizzes at navigation."

We looked meaningfully at each other.

"Anyway, I've traced these telephone calls they've made to numbers in Tampa," Jack continued. "There are a lot of calls to a certain Al Khader or El Kader or Al Kaderi. The names are hard to keep track of because they are almost identical. I'm also tracking the license plates of the luxury vehicles that pass through these guys' hands. I believe they're in on a money-making scheme where stolen cars are repainted and shipped out from the port of Tampa to the Middle East. Once over there, they're sold for big money—money which is used to finance the mullahs in Iran or the Houthis, for instance."

"Jack, this is incredible!" I cried. "What do the ICE people think? What do you think about this, Jill?"

"Well, Jack is supposed to go to the ICE office in Tampa next week to discuss his findings. They seem to be taking him seriously." She sounded a little skeptical but proud, and I was glad they were showing a united front on this. It could be big!

"Yeah, and if I'm really on to something, there is a reward. And we could sure use the money!" Jack wore a happy grin.

I hoped he was right. Right in every way possible about catching the bad guys and claiming a reward. Terrorist financing seems to have gotten so sophisticated these days. I hoped Jack wasn't chasing a pipe dream here. For all of his street smarts, it was one of his specialties when easy money dangled in front of his eyes. After 9/11, it was important for everyone to be aware that the world was a much more sophisticated and dangerous place. And if Jack had uncovered nefarious activities of any kind, sitting at his computer screen hour after hour trying to connect the dots, then there damn well should be a reward. And a good one.

CHAPTER THREE

"Lunch on Pineapple Avenue"

With our summer vacation in France quickly fading into the background, life moved on. Sam and I settled back into our winter lives and routines in sunny Sarasota. Sam returned to work at the hydraulic factory on an artificial lake near Sarasota airport. It was one of the few light industries in Sarasota, which was mostly a vacation destination whose economy was based on tourism. The company was very successful, and there was a lot of overtime, and Sam liked working there. The workforce was a potpourri of various nationalities, Hispanic, Thai, Vietnamese, Florida 'crackers', otherwise known as native Floridians, and my Sam, who was from Romania. They all exchanged dishes and recipes over lunchtime, trying not to drop too many crumbs into the hydraulic fluid.

Meanwhile, I went back to my volunteer job at the Orchid Research Center of the Selby Gardens, where I spent a few days each week translating a work about New Caledonian orchids from French into English. Most orchids were purple, so I used all my ingenuity to come up with different names for the shades, such as violet, mauve, lavender, etc. My colleagues were very nice, and I enjoyed my time there.

The Orchid Research Center building, where I worked, was small with old-fashioned jalousie windows. It was a bit run-down in a genteel, old-Floridian way. Spanish moss dripped from the trees by the parking area. The nearby Selby Garden and mansion, on the other hand, was a beautiful place and beautifully maintained. It was right on Sarasota Bay. The Selby family had been some of the heirs to the Standard Oil fortune, and they had donated their property to the city. The garden housed a big collection of orchids in a special greenhouse. There was a winding path along the water through stands of tall Japanese bamboo, where the trees with their many nodes made music as they swayed in the breeze off the bay. It was a lovely walk, and I often went there with a sandwich at lunchtime to sit under the bodhi tree that was planted right at a point of the garden looking out on the bay, an idyllic spot. A bodhi tree is the variety of tree under which the Buddha sat in India when he attained enlightenment. I sat, but, unfortunately, was not necessarily enlightened. The gardens were home to many tropical and subtropical plants from all over the world. One of the most unusual was the titan arum. When the giant flower bloomed, it gave off a noxious odor, very like rotten fish! Although it seems counterintuitive, it was a big tourist attraction when it blossomed every few years or so, and brought a lot of visitors to the gardens.

My first day back as a volunteer ended with a treat. My friend, Summer Bogdonavich, heard I was back in town and invited me for lunch. We were meeting at her favorite restaurant, the Wildflower Café, at the intersection of

Pineapple and Orange, not far from the gardens. It wasn't always easy to find a parking place around there. The area was very popular, with its cute boutiques and sidewalk eateries catering to the ladies-who-lunch crowd; I'm happy to admit I'm one of them.

This time, I was lucky and found an empty spot right away. After several vacations in France, it always amused me how big the parking spaces were in Sarasota. Each one was equal to two spaces in the towns near Montpezat de Quercy, like Caussade or Cahors. Most parking lots in Florida were head-first, pull-in, since there was plenty of land to spare even in the city centers. It was just the opposite of the little cities in France, where space was at a premium and one's parking skills had to be well-honed to back in and squeeze between cars, ornamental trees, iron barriers, and cement barrier posts, or whatever else was adjacent. Not only did Sarasotans drive very big vehicles, but the population, young and old, had pretty much forgotten how to parallel park.

My friend, Summer, was already there and waved me over to an outdoor table. Thankfully, it had an umbrella, as it was a very hot afternoon. I had met Summer at yoga class a couple of winters ago. She was originally from up north like me, but she had been in Florida for much longer.

Sarasota was a bigger city than Summer's former haunts. It was culturally very rich since it boasted the Sarasota Opera, the ballet, several theaters, and the Sarasota Arts Center, not to mention the jewel in the city's crown, The Ringling Museum of Art.

I sat down and said, "You look great, Summer. New haircut? I love it!"

"Do you really? I think it's very short, but Evin over at 'Heads Up' said it was perfect for my face shape." She sounded very happy with the choice.

We ordered salads and glasses of Sauvignon Blanc. Summer asked about my work at the Orchid Research Center. We exchanged news about my Sam and her partner, Charlie. Summer's two sons were doing well, as was my family. Summer asked about my niece, Melanie, whom she had met once or twice. Since I didn't have any children, Melanie was like a daughter to me. She was my sister's eldest and my favorite, because we were so much alike. We were both art lovers. She was now in a degree program at the prestigious Ringling School of Art—no relation to The Ringling Museum. Summer had accompanied me to a couple of Melanie's exhibits, and like me, was duly impressed by her cutting-edge photography.

Fall was my favorite season in South Florida. It was so pleasant sitting at our table on the little sidewalk, the restaurant's flower boxes shielding us from the pedestrians who were busy window shopping only a few feet away. The muted conversation from the other tables was punctuated by an occasional tinkle of laughter. Our salads were delicious and loaded with pieces of grouper.

As we sipped at our wine, I could just spy the vine-covered facade of the historic Burns Court Cinema from our table. Burns Court was the independent movie house in town and showed all the latest and most artistic films. It was part of a little sliver of a neighborhood left intact from the 1920s. Most of Sarasota was brand new, modern development, and although very sleek and good-looking, precious pockets of older neighborhoods lent a contrast from a gentler era that I thought heightened the interest of both.

I was just about to ask for the bill when Summer recognized a friend passing by our table. She had long, blond-streaked hair, and her skin was a honey tone that looked truly authentic and not created with tanning creams. Summer called out to her, "Marybelle How are you? Don't you recognize me with my new hairdo?"

"Why, Summer! I didn't see you at all. I was preoccupied. How are you, honey?" I may have been mistaken, but I thought Marybelle had a hint of an accent. Being an ex-French teacher and bilingual, I find my ear is very sensitive to diction, and the way she said "honey" definitely had a Caribbean lilt.

"I'm doing great," Summer said, then, "Oh, where are my manners? Let me introduce you to each other. Marybelle Thomson, I'd like you to meet my good friend, Barbara Waldheim. She's just come back to Sarasota for the winter. Normally, we lose her to the south of France every summer. She has a home there."

"Pleased to meet you, Barbara," Marybelle smiled broadly, and sounded as if she meant it. We shook hands warmly across the table. "Well, I should get back." She nodded to a table with several people sipping coffee and having an animated conversation. "We're discussing the arrangements for this year's Sarasota Film Festival. We're looking for volunteers to be on our committee." A sudden gleam lit her eye. "Barbara, since you're just back in town, might you be interested?"

"I'd be very interested," I told her. "I love the movies, and I'd love to get involved."

"Then I'll need your phone number," Marybelle said, taking out her own phone. "I'll give you a call one day soon."

———

That evening, I met up with Sam for dinner back at my house. The place was all cleaned up, and order had been restored. All traces of Waylan Cooper had finally been expunged. The weird stone carving was banished outside, leaning against a wall of the shed, half hidden by a croton bush.

Our custom was to start the meal with a glass of wine and a baguette cut into rounds that we dipped in Sam's signature concoction: a sauce of extra virgin olive oil mixed with various herbs, spices, and an *essential* ingredient—paprika from Szeged, a town near Sam's birthplace in Romania. Maria Callas as Carmen played on the stereo. Sam hummed and trilled along with her as he turned the red snapper over on the George Foreman grill. He had also prepared an Israeli salad, another of his special dishes, that was waiting in the refrigerator.

It wasn't long before the fish was served and flaking on our forks. Diced cucumbers, red onion, parsley, and tomatoes tossed in olive oil and lemon juice nestled on our salad plates. As we ate, I told him how the Sarasota Film Festival organizers were looking for interested volunteers and that I might be invited to join one of the Film Festival committees. He agreed that it would be fun to be involved, even on the periphery.

Sam sipped his wine thoughtfully. "What about your niece?"

"Melanie?"

"Wouldn't she love something like that? She would certainly be interested in being involved with a community film event like this festival. Plus, you could spend some quality time together in between her classes at the Ringling School of Art."

"Sam Spitz, what an excellent idea!" I was surprised that I hadn't thought of it myself. "A truly excellent idea," I repeated, feeling pleased.

Changing the subject, Sam continued, "Listen, Barbara. I read an interesting article in *The Tribune* over lunch hour. Did you see it? It was about The Ringling Museum. I saved the newspaper for you. Here, take a look."

He reached over the countertop for the folded newspaper. "It says The Ringling Museum is in big trouble. Their finances are shot. The board of governors is fighting among themselves to place the blame on each other for the problems."

"No kidding," I said drily. "I read a story online about that, too. Somebody at the Selby Gardens mentioned innuendoes of financial impropriety among the Ringling board of trustees."

Sam asked if I had seen the announcement of some new "Behind the Scenes" classes at The Ringling. "They're right in your alley," he told me.

"*Up* your alley, Sam, but an excellent use of an American expression," I said, smiling at him.

I found it so endearing the way Sam sometimes messed up American idiomatic expressions. He spoke Romanian, Hungarian, Hebrew, English, and some French, so I figured he was entitled to make a mistake on a preposition here or there.

"What's up my alley?"

Sam scanned the article in the paper. He read "The Ringling is offering 'Behind the Scenes' classes to try to heighten public awareness about what the museum does, of its importance to the community ..."

"And, of course, to raise money," he finished with a knowing smile.

"Well, everybody needs money." I reached for the paper. "Let me see the article, please. That kind of thing is right *up* my alley. Thanks, Sam."

He rose and began to clear away the dinner things as I looked at the paper, head bowed, lost in the article.

"Thanks for showing me this, Sam," I said as I pulled myself back to the present. "I'll definitely sign up for one of these classes, and I'll talk to Melanie about volunteering for the Film Festival. You're on fire with great ideas tonight."

"No, dessert is on fire." With a huge smile, he returned to the table with a flaming dish of Bananas Foster and two bowls of ice cream.

CHAPTER FOUR

The first meeting of the Sarasota Film Festival Committee was to take place at Sanderling, a private enclave of houses on Siesta Key where Marybelle lived. On the afternoon of the meeting, I collected Melanie, and we drove south on Tamiami Trail to the bridge over to Siesta Key. The Tamiami Trail was the old Seminole and Calusa Indian path. It ran along both the eastern and western coasts of the State of Florida. In Sarasota, the Trail was now a four-lane road, US 41. When I got to the drawbridge over to Siesta Key, it was open. We waited at the blinking lights before crossing to the island as a tall-masted sailboat passed underneath the uplifted roadway.

"By the way, your aviator sunglasses are cool," I told my young passenger. "You look just right for the committee meeting."

Melanie chuckled. 'Yeah, I wanted to fit in with the Sanderling crowd, and "Vroom Vroom" says these reflectors protect your eyes. He and I are planning to head to Tampa this weekend, to Ybor City, to do some club-hopping."

Vroom Vroom was Melanie's boyfriend, Vernon Verdon. Sam and I liked Vroom Vroom and could see his good points. He was a tall, skinny young man who loved motorcycles. They had been dating for about a year now. He had a fine education and held a responsible position in the start-up software company he had helped found. Yet Sam and I couldn't help but wonder if he and Melanie were really meant for one another in the long run. Only time would tell.

"That sounds nice, honey," I told Melanie, thinking to myself that Ybor City and its clubs were about the only interests my niece and I didn't have in common. It was great to be young. The drawbridge slowly lowered, and we followed a line of cars over the roadway to Siesta Key and turned left toward Turtle Beach and our destination.

Sanderling was a private neighborhood. I stopped at the gatehouse and gave my name. The guard directed me the short distance ahead to the clubhouse on the beachfront with a polite reminder of the speed limit. I drove along a roadbed made of crushed seashells under a canopy of live oak trees, icons of the old South, their branches dripping with Spanish moss and creating dappled light on the shell road, which crunched softly under our tires. A blue heron fished silently in the shallow water of the lagoon, and the cry of a gull filled the air. Hidden among the greenery, I caught glimpses of some of the houses peeking out along the winding road. The Sanderling enclave was decidedly old-Florida style, tropical, but in a naturally ecological way.

We parked on the sand in front of the clubhouse, a handsome, modern structure that was mostly open to the air.

At the entrance, a plaque said that Paul Rudolph, Dean of the Yale School of Architecture, designed the building in 1959.

"Very classy," Melanie crooned with delight. "I read a paper on him recently. He was from the Sarasota School of Architecture, like Paul Twitchell. They were both deeply influenced by Frank Lloyd Wright's ideas."

"Is that so?" I said, amazed as usual by the breadth of Melanie's art historical knowledge. This was her general area of expertise, however. She was working toward her master's in art with a specialization in photography.

Melanie elaborated, sensing my interest. "The two were able to turn some of their more ambitious designs into reality when they snagged several commissions to build in clean lines that harmonized with the low-lying coastal landscape around Sarasota. I read about their experimentation with new materials from the 1950s, like plywood that was inexpensive but not so well-suited to the South Florida climate. It warped in the rain and humidity."

"Oh dear. Luckily for us, the Sanderling clubhouse appears to be solid," I mused, making Melanie giggle.

The committee meeting was already in progress, so we quietly took our seats. Marybelle caught my eye from the front of the room and gave me a friendly nod. She and twenty or so people were listening to a man explain our group's assignments for the film festival. The speaker was Marybelle's husband, Peter Thomson. Together, they owned and operated Thomson's MareSol Properties.

Aha, so that's where I'd seen Marybelle before. It had been nagging at me since Summer introduced us that I knew her from somewhere else. Mind you, Sarasota wasn't that big, and it was entirely possible we'd bumped into one another at some event or other. Now I realized it wasn't that at all. Her photos appeared in glossy, local lifestyle magazines alongside her husband, advertising their business ventures. Peter Thomson was the developer who was changing the face of Siesta Key with his high-end housing projects. Marybelle was responsible for decorating the gorgeous show houses, enticing well-heeled clients to sign up to buy one.

Peter stated that the film festival would take place three months from now, in early February. He said that most of the planning had started a year in advance and had been handled by a professional staff working out of their little cottage on Fruitville Road. Even so, there was an important role for the volunteers who would be an integral part of making the film festival a successful event. Just as Marybelle's sincerity had struck me at the restaurant on Pineapple, her husband also came across as warmer and more accessible than I had expected from his public image.

My attention was drawn away from Peter for a moment by the beautiful view of the Gulf of Mexico from the open-air clubhouse. Most of the beachfront on Siesta Key was a flat expanse of white, powdery sand sloping very gently to the water. Great for little children since the water stays shallow for a long way out. This powdered sugar sand was a special attribute of the barrier island's beaches. It had washed all the way down here from the Appalachian Mountains over many millennia and contained a very high concentration of silica. The silica conducted heat down deep into the sand, which meant that Siesta Key beachgoers never burned their feet.

At Sanderling's beach, the ocean surf sprayed over the only shoal of rocks on Siesta Key. A wooden staircase allowed bathers to enter the water and swim out to the rocks. The scene looked enticing, and to my mind, European in style, like Capri or le Cap d'Antibes, more than the other Siesta beaches, beautiful though they were.

Melanie brought me out of my reverie with a gentle nudge.

She nodded discreetly to a beautiful woman sitting to one side. "That's Caterina Alvarez. She's an up-and-coming fashion designer, and I *love* her stuff."

"Who?"

"This is one of her scarves." Melanie fluttered a cheerful piece of fabric at me. "Vernon bought it for me."

"Oh." I was impressed with Caterina. "It's lovely."

I'd admired the scarf earlier when Melanie had first jumped in the car. I cast a sideways glance at Caterina. She sat ramrod straight, her light brown hair pulled severely back from her pretty features into a long, braided ponytail, very practical in Sarasota's mostly hot, humid weather. This young woman, however, made the hairdo look distinctly high style. Her jeans and simple top hung just so on her fashion-model frame. She was wearing high-heeled sandals and an unusual but handsome asymmetrical necklace. My gaze must not have been as discreet as I'd hoped, for she suddenly looked over at us. Her eyes were a beautiful sapphire blue.

"She's gorgeous," Melanie whispered.

"What a lovely young woman," I agreed. "No wonder she works in fashion. She certainly has a lot of style." I'd already noticed the volunteers in general were a younger crowd than often found in Sarasota, which had a big winter population of retirees. This pleased me as it meant Melanie would not feel out of place.

Caterina smiled at us. Another moment of radiance as she had a truly beautiful smile. We smiled back and then turned our full attention back to Peter, who was explaining that this volunteer group was going to split up into committees to organize some of the parties happening around the film festival.

As for the festival itself, the foreign film entries would be screened either at the Regal Multiplex or the Burns Court

Cinema for two weeks before the winner was announced, to give people a chance to pick an audience favorite. The mainstream, big box-office movies would also be shown to the public, and a jury of former winners would choose this year's awardees. We were told the exact line-up of films and star speakers was still a secret. It would be fun to see the selected film entries before the rest of the country and vote on our favorites, but the big excitement would be provided by the chance to see, or even rub shoulders with, actors like Cillian Murphy. He had appeared one year at the Sarasota Film Festival before he won his Oscar for *Oppenheimer*, or Alicia Silverstone from *Clueless* and *Batman Returns*.

Peter Thomson told us that Tom Selleck from the TV shows *Magnum, P.I.* and *Blue Bloods* might be the master of ceremonies at one of the parties. He had a house on Casey Key in Sarasota and was a fixture of the city's social scene. Or maybe Ted Danson from *Cheers* would do some of the honors.

It was all rather exciting, and the thought of being involved turned my head a little. There were no brushes with celebrities like this in Montpezat de Quercy. The closest equivalent was when former Queen Margrethe of Denmark took up summer residence at her chateau in Cahors, about thirty kilometers away.

The larger meeting broke up, and we were divided into subcommittees. I was delighted when Marybelle came over to say hello and asked to meet the stylish young woman accompanying me.

"This is Melanie, my niece. She would like to work with us on one of the sub-committees. I brought her along with me today."

"Nice to meet you, honey. It's always great to have young blood."

I was curious and asked Marybelle about her lovely accent.

It turned out our committee chairperson was born on the Caribbean Island of Saint Kitts and had moved to Sarasota as a teenager.

Melanie and I ended up on different teams for the various events. We separated into little clusters in the main area to plan. Our group voted to meet the following week at the subcommittee chairperson's house to get down to business. Marybelle was elected head of my subcommittee, which was great with me. That way, I was acquainted with at least one person, but I would no doubt get to know some of the others as time went by.

Peter adjourned the main meeting and thanked everyone for coming. The clubhouse emptied quickly as the Sanderling Bridge Club was waiting on the sidelines to start their game.

"I'm on the same team as Caterina," Melanie said happily, settling into the passenger seat. "Our event is a luncheon for donors at a French restaurant up on the North Trail near The Ringling Museum. What's yours?"

"I'm working on the barbecue for foreign films at the Regal, but at least Marybelle is with me, so I know somebody. What's this Caterina like?" I asked, smiling at the enthusiasm Melanie had for the designer.

"Very quiet, but nice. We had a short chat about the building. Turns out she's a Paul Rudolph fan, too. She studied at the Instituto Europeo di Design in Barcelona." Melanie sounded impressed, so I was, too. "Our team is meeting up next week at her work studio," she continued.

"Ours, too, only at Marybelle and Peter's house."

Melanie reached over and gave my arm a squeeze. "Thanks for asking me along, Aunt Barbara. This is great. I'm going to love working on this festival. I can easily fit it in around my university work."

I smiled. Those were the best words I could have heard. I

was looking forward to the festival immensely, as well. This was my type of project, and sharing it with my niece made it even better for me.

Since this was going so well, on our drive home, I proposed that Melanie attend one of The Ringling's "Behind the Scenes" workshops with her old auntie.

Melanie was looking out the passenger side window of my sporty Toyota 86 at the passing housing complexes as we drove along Siesta Drive toward her dorm. Turning toward me, she cried, "It's amazing how we're interested in the same stuff, Aunt Barbara! Those courses caught my attention, too. You are really trouble—keeping me from my school work. I'm going to have to give you a talking to. Seriously, email me the info, will you, and I'll take a look and see if one of the dates fits into my schedule. I sure would like to get a peek at what it's like behind the scenes of The Ringling. I'll work it in somehow and let you know."

CHAPTER FIVE

"Hydraulics and Hotdogs by the Bay"

One of the perks of Sam's hydraulic valve company was the annual picnic they held for employees. The management always picked an interesting venue in Sarasota, like the historic Powel-Crosley Mansion or the Classic Car Museum. In that way, guests like me had extra motivation to attend the party, and employees had something else to discuss besides shop talk. Some of the awkwardness of fraternizing with the front office bosses was eliminated by sharing an experience together. This year, the site of the company picnic was to be The Ringling Museum. I was very happy about that because I loved going there to see the paintings, and now I was looking forward to their behind-the-scenes class with Melanie.

The museum was founded by John and Mable Ringling of the Ringling Brothers Barnum & Bailey Circus fame. John

Ringling was the youngest of the seven brothers from Baraboo, Wisconsin, who started the circus at the turn of the century. He was the brother who was in charge of logistics, and by the 1920s, he was enormously rich. He had almost unlimited means, and the showman that he was, he thought big when it came to his vacation residence in Florida. He already had a mansion on Fifth Avenue in New York City when he decided on a winter residence in Florida, a reproduction of a Venetian palazzo for himself and his wife on their enormous property on Sarasota Bay. He named it Cà d'Zan, which means John's House in Venetian dialect. His and Mable's gondolas were kept moored to the gaily painted posts anchored in the clear water off the mansion's terrace just as if they were in the Grand Canal in Venice.

The couple also needed a place to store the enormous art collection they had amassed on their travels, so they built a museum near their mansion. There were twenty-one galleries of Medieval, Renaissance, and Baroque artwork that the Ringlings had brought back from Europe over seventy years ago. The museum was in a grand, neoclassical building with two long wings that bordered a landscaped, sculpture-filled courtyard dominated by a life-size replica of Michelangelo's *David* from Florence.

There was also plenty of room on the twenty-acre waterfront property to reconstruct a jewel of an Italian Renaissance theater purchased in its entirety in Asolo, Italy. The theater was located between the mansion and the museum, not far from Mable's extensive rose garden. In addition, as the years went by, a little circus curiosity museum was added that featured items from early circus acts, like the cannon that shot out Hugo Zacchini, the "human cannonball," as he was billed, and memorabilia from sad-eyed Emmet Kelly, the world-famous clown. A few of the original circus wagons were on display, decorated with Egyptian pyramids and pharaoh motifs, or the temples of South India with their pantheon of fantastic gods—wonders of the world which amazed and attracted customers in those less sophisticated times before television—as they rolled into towns and cities across America. Some of the Tarzan-like costumes worn by big cat tamer Gunter Goebel Williams were shown, along with a valuable collection of vintage advertising posters ballyhooing the circus's arrival in town.

The property was landscaped with many giant banyan trees, just like the Ringling's friends Thomas Edison and Henry Ford had planted on their own Florida estates down the coast in Fort Myers.

In Sarasota and nearby Venice, Florida, the thousands of circus employees had a winter hiatus from traveling while they rehearsed new acts and got things in order for the upcoming season. There was competition from other circuses, and Ringling Brothers had to keep up in order to bill themselves "the Greatest Show on Earth."

Those heady days were long gone now. John Ringling died in 1936 at age 47, and Mable died a few years before him in 1929. The Ringlings left a lasting legacy. His museum and art collections were a cultural treasure, and the estate and its grounds were one of the city's biggest assets.

Or were they? John Ringling willed his creation, plus a 1.2-million-dollar endowment, to the people of the state of Florida, not directly to Sarasota. He was personally almost bankrupt at his death, and his gift was entangled with debts. The state fought with John Ringling's creditors and eventually prevailed. Even after winning ownership in court, Florida did little to manage the endowment or maintain the property, while the Sarasota community felt it was the state's responsibility to support the museum. By the late 1990s, the Ringling mansion was falling apart, as were the exterior footpaths and roads. The museum had a serious roof leak, and the security systems were wholly inadequate to protect the collection. The Asolo theater building the Ringlings imported from Italy, was condemned, and the 1.2 million dollar endowment had only grown to two million dollars from 1936 to 1996, a period of 60 years! A pitiable rate of return!

These were the problems that had been undermining The Ringling for decades before the day of Sam's company picnic at the museum.

When Sam and I arrived at the event, I was met with a big letdown. Our event wasn't taking place in the museum itself. Instead, our tables were set up on a scrubby stretch of vacant, sandy ground near the back of the courtyard wall, though we *were* close to the bay, and the grilled hot dogs and hamburgers were tasty and kept on coming. Sam introduced me to some of his coworkers, and we drank beer out of big, red plastic cups and made light conversation. It was a hot, humid day, unusual for October, a month that was often more temperate. I was talking with Ellen, a colleague of Sam's. She had been in the testing department since before Sam had joined the company and was friends with everybody.

"Have you ever been to the museum, Ellen?" I asked her.

"Nah. All those old master paintings aren't my thing. I've been inside the mansion, though. It's really something. Those Ringlings sure knew how to live. Have you seen that big organ they had in the living room? The guide said they had some crazy parties."

"Really," I said. "An organ? That's interesting. I guess rich people had to have a big organ in those days for prestige. I saw another one at a Rockefeller house up north. You know, the museum is very impressive, too. I thought at first that it wasn't serious because the Ringlings were circus people, but this summer Sam and I were in Paris and saw one of their paintings on loan at the Luxembourg Palace."

"Yeah," Ellen sniffed. "That's right, you guys go to France a lot, don't you? It sounds nice," she said, wistfully.

Warming to my subject, I told her that this summer we had been to a prestigious show of the artist Titian, who painted in the 1500s in Venice. He painted a lot of portraits, especially of redheads. "I was walking through the Luxembourg Palace exhibition, and imagine my surprise to see a painting from here. It was *La Sultana Rossa,* painted in 1560, and was on loan from The Ringling Museum." If I expected an equal measure of enthusiasm from Ellen, I was sadly mistaken.

"That's something alright," she said, her eyes darting around, looking desperately but not finding someone else to talk to.

I pressed on gamely as this sort of thing fascinated me. "You know, The Ringling is famous as a research center, too. It's published ..."

At this point, Ellen waved like she was drowning to Hector, another tester, and headed off in his direction, mouthing to me a silent "See ya." She obviously wasn't a fan of the arts.

Next, I ran into Nancy, who worked in the main office and was rumored to be having an affair with Charles Stutz, the company president and head engineer. We got to talking about the art collection, and I repeated my story about the Ringling painting Sam and I had seen on loan in Paris at the *Titian and His Redheads* exhibition.

Nancy leaned in closer to me and said conspiratorially, "I heard The Ringling Museum isn't in too good shape, financially, I mean. The board must have run out of money or something. Do you see those cracks in the wall over there?"

I turned to look at a long concrete wall, which I recognized as the exterior of one of the two long wings of the museum courtyard extending toward Sarasota Bay. The Ringling was built in a U shape with two long legs reaching out to the Intracoastal Waterway. The entrance and the main part of the museum were at the bottom of the U, and the galleries continued along both legs of the U, with the sculpture courtyard in the empty middle part. To cross over from one leg to the other without going back to the bottom of U, there was an elevated walkway, or balustrade, connecting the two legs. In the middle of this balustrade stood a life-size replica of Michelangelo's famous statue of *David,* overlooking the other sculptures arranged in the garden below.

"That cement work of the wall there doesn't look good," Nancy continued. "And why do you think we're allowed to picnic on the grounds? They need to make money fast."

"Oh, okay." I knew the layout of the museum, but I had never stood outside observing the exterior of this courtyard wall before. As Nancy remarked, it was badly in need of repair. I had noticed the sidewalks and steps up to the museum were cracked and bumpy, but I had just accepted it as the usual state of affairs. It had been like that for a long time. Sam came over and joined us.

"It's time for the raffle, ladies," he said. Sam called all women *ladies.* I didn't mind. I liked it. "Here's the ticket I picked out of the hat. I'm number 21, but I never win anything." Charles Stutz, company president, stepped up to the microphone, and everybody applauded. He had an easygoing personality and was generally well-liked. It was time for the drawing. The prizes were displayed on the table in front of him: an electric popcorn popper, a gift certificate to Applebee's, and a fancy barbecue grill.

"Come on, lucky number twenty-one," Sam cheered for himself.

Mr. Stutz drew out a number. "Twenty-one. Who's got number twenty-one?" Sam's face burst into a delighted grin. "Over here, Charlie. That's my number!" Sam went up and shook the president's hand. He got first pick of the prizes and selected the grill. He was awfully pleased. We went home from the picnic feeling that it had been a very successful day.

CHAPTER SIX

"La Sultana Rossa"

Two days later, I was back at The Ringling, this time with Melanie to attend our "Behind the Scenes" class. It would be interesting to hear a museum curator explain the latest techniques in art restoration. The one-time, late afternoon session wasn't very costly, and we considered the payment as a small contribution to the museum's finances. The word was out that The Ringling Museum was on its uppers and risked running out of operating funds. The newspaper reported that there were buckets in The Ringling's Venetian-style mansion to catch the rainwater. As I'd already seen for myself at Sam's company picnic, the cement walkways were cracked and crumbling. Mable Ringling's rose garden had fallen into ruin. The museum was poorly lit, and the galleries were not well-maintained. What on earth had happened to Mable and John Ringling's considerable endowment? That's what everyone was asking. Meanwhile, the board of governors pointed fingers at each other for the fiscal mismanagement.

It was proposed by a local newspaper editorial that artwork be sold to make up the shortfall, but the board chairman responded that John Ringling stipulated in his will that no artwork be sold. The collection must be kept together in perpetuity; otherwise, it would be disbanded and distributed to Ringling's remaining heirs. What a mess.

I'd arranged to meet Melanie in the museum parking lot. I was lounging in the shade under the walkway canopy, enjoying the breeze off Sarasota Bay, when I heard the throaty roar of a motorcycle engine. Surely it couldn't be—

It was.

Melanie, on a shiny, brand-new motorcycle, swooped to a stop beside me, flipped up her visor, and gave me the cheekiest grin. "Hello, Aunt Barbara."

"Have you bought a bike?" My jaw dropped. I knew her boyfriend Vernon, aka Vroom Vroom, was crazy about motorcycles, but never suspected Melanie had caught the bug this bad.

"Isn't she a beauty?" She swung her leg over to dismount and patted the tank. "She's a Honda 500, and I call her Izzy, after Isadora Duncan."

"Oh. Um, yes, she's a beauty all right." I felt a little uncertain, especially as Izzy was named for a famous accident victim. "I hope you're safe on it, Melanie."

"She's an excellent choice for new riders. A great first bike. Vernon helped me buy it."

Melanie pried off her helmet. "I took a safety course and then got my driver's licence three weeks ago. I didn't say anything because I wanted to surprise you and Sam." She looked so proud that my anxiety abated a little. Melanie was a clever kid; she always knew what she was doing. I needed to cut her some slack. After all, she had her mother to give her grief about this latest development. And I couldn't see Sam being too enthused either; he was very protective of Melanie. So, I decided to be the super cool aunt and said, "I'm sure you and Vernon will have a fabulous time tooling around on your bikes." That earned me a hug. "Thank you, Aunt Barbara. Mom's being such a pain about it."

"Oh, you know your mom. She'll chill out eventually." My sister, Amy, was a worrywart. It was only natural that the thought of her daughter on a motorcycle kept her up at night. I, on the other hand, could be the cool aunt.

We linked arms and headed for the museum entrance, leaving behind the beautiful sunshine of the late afternoon. Once inside the foyer, we were escorted along with about a dozen women and one man through a staff-only door to the administrative wing that housed the offices and conference rooms. This area was unknown to me, although I had visited the museum many times on my own, as well as on several guided tours.

We were ushered into one of the smaller meeting rooms and seated in a semi-circle around our instructor, who introduced herself in a very British accent as Antonia Wexford. Ms. Wexford was the opposite of a chic "Sloane Ranger" like Princess Diana or a tall, bohemian Brit with the flair and style to make Portobello Road vintage finds look fashionable. She was a small, compact, older woman. Prim and proper, her hairdo was styled in a stiff bouffant. She was wearing a tweed suit (in Florida!) and sensible shoes. She reminded me of the late Queen Elizabeth in that she was even carrying an old-fashioned, snap-closure handbag. She explained to us that she had come to The Ringling from the prestigious Courtauld Museum in London, and before that, she had worked with the Royal Art Collection at both Windsor Castle and Buckingham

Palace. In short, she knew her stuff and was not to be trifled with. She certainly gave off no-nonsense vibrations. As she introduced herself, our comportment improved as if we were at a palace reception, and we sat up straighter in our chairs. We were excited.

Ms. Wexford opened her lecture with a slide show displaying one of the most ambitious examples of recent art restoration projects—the Sistine Chapel ceiling by Michelangelo at the Vatican. Slides illustrated the before and after of the extensive modern renovation of the ceiling frescoes carried out starting in the 1980s and into the '90s. What a difference the restoration made! Damage caused by water leaking from the floor above the chapel had been erased, and the dark saltpetre accretions on the frescoes were removed. In a similar fashion, the grime from five hundred years of candle wax and soot from burning candles, which had obscured and dimmed the colors, was no longer in evidence. In some areas, structural cracks from the building shifting over the centuries had created gaps in the figures. These fault lines had been filled in.

As beautiful and impressive as the *before* slides were, the *after* slides revealed a dazzlingly fresh and rejuvenated artwork. Ms. Wexford explained to us that the efforts at conserving the Sistine Chapel had been going on for good or ill since 1625, when a cleaning was carried out by rubbing the ceiling with bread. Seventy years later, removal of the accretion of soot and grime trapped in the oily deposits of the first restoration was attempted by rubbing the frescoes with sponges dipped in Greek wine. "Techniques have changed considerably since then," the art historian assured us with a wink so broad she lost her balance. As she lurched forward dangerously, she grabbed onto the slide projector just in time to prevent it and herself from overturning.

Melanie and I exchanged shocked glances, wondering if Ms. Wexford herself hadn't been dipping into the Greek wine at lunch. There was a collective gasp from the audience. "Are you alright, Ms. Wexford?" someone asked.

"What do you mean? Tickety boo," our tipsy instructor replied, brushing off the little incident.

A hand raised. The woman on my right said, "I thought this was supposed to be a behind-the-scenes class about The Ringling. Why are we talking about the Sistine Chapel?" The art historian gave her challenger a haughty stare.

"You colonials certainly are in a hurry," enunciated Ms. Wexford in her clipped British English, barely managing to control her annoyance at being rushed along. "Very well," our lecturer continued, flipping through her notes. "Let us talk about some of the latest techniques in art restoration today. The field is in constant evolution. The goal is to use the newest techniques available and still preserve the original intent and spirit of the work. This is another aspic, *hiccup,* I mean to say, aspect of the restoration process, which demands intense study and investigation before any work can get underway." *Aspic!* A few people tittered. Our group of a dozen art lovers started to get restless. Antonia Wexford was losing control of her audience. *How are the mighty fallen!*

Melanie raised her hand. "So, no more solutions and Q-tips® in the restoration process used here at The Ringling?" my niece asked, though a little lightheartedly. I suspected she already knew the answer but was trying to help Antonia Wexford get back on track.

It seemed to work because the curator projected a slide from The Ringling Museum collection on the screen in front of us.

"This is Titian's *La Sultana Rossa,* a fascinating portrait of a beautiful, red red-haired, young woman. You'll note she's wearing a high conical hat, which is decorated with a splendid oriental jewel like the Indian maharajas wore on their turbans. See how she's dressed in a luxurious gown and holds a furry little animal like a mink on her lap."

"I saw this painting last summer at the Titian exhibit in Paris," I said.

"Well, aren't you the lucky one," Ms. Wexford drawled sardonically. "I'd loved to have seen that show. But *I* didn't, and *they* didn't, and *we* don't care!" she snapped, putting me in my place.

"Now, *La Sultana Rossa* is controversial for several reasons. But first, what do you think the title means?"

I wanted to say, but I didn't dare open my mouth.

"People think it means the red-headed woman in Italian, but the verdict is out. Although the beauty in the portrait has red hair and Titian was known for painting red-haired subjects, some experts attest that the painting is instead called *La Sultana Russa*. Why? Because we think it is a portrait of a Ukrainian concubine of Suleiman the Magnificent, the longest-reigning sultan of the Ottoman Empire. He had many concubines, but this young woman was his favorite and became his wife.

"Now, two other controversies about this work: is this painting a copy of an earlier Titian painting, which is now lost but documented as having existed? Did Titian paint the canvas at all, or was it the apprentices in his studio? As you might easily imagine, when a painting is 470 years old, has been sold and resold, and the documentation is missing or lost, absolute certainty about its authorship and even the identity of the subject of the portrait is open to debate."

We in the audience murmured appreciatively, thinking over the knotty problems surrounding this portrait. Ms. Wexford was winning us over again.

"As the young woman pointed out," Ms Wexford said, indicating Melanie, "there is no further need for old-fashioned cotton buds and turpentine to clean a painting. There's an exciting new technique allowing us to remove dirt particles in the old varnish without touching the paint layers underneath. The technique uses light energy and is called laser ablation. No solvent is involved, which eliminates any unpredictable side effects. In addition, multi-spectral imaging and X-ray fluorescence are now so precise that only the dirt particles coating the paint are removed. So, no need to repaint certain areas of the canvas. Heavy repainting could totally change the appearance of an artwork, making attribution more difficult.

"But unfortunately, we cannot employ this cutting-edge technique to answer some of these questions here at The Ringling." Saying this, Antonia Wexford became very sad, and her face fell. Dejected, she sat down, slumped over, in a chair next to the slide projector. *Whatever happened to the famous British stiff upper lip?* A lace hanky appeared in her hand from out of her purse, and she dabbed at her eyes.

We in the audience hardly knew how to react to the drama unfolding before us. If we had expected a somewhat dry lecture, what we were getting was more like a tragicomedy. It certainly wasn't boring. We waited to see what shoe would drop next.

Ms. Wexford pulled herself together and went on. "Due to budget constraints, The Ringling Museum does not have the facilities to do further research into the mysteries swirling around this painting. Not all establishments have access to the same level of technology. Some technical departments are very advanced, and others ... well, struggle." I wondered if this was a reference to The Ringling Museum's financial woes. *If the façade was literally falling apart, what hope did the laboratories have of snagging the best scientific equipment?*

She began to wind down the workshop. "Before we go to take a look at The Ringling's technical department, where we do what restoration we can, let me remind you that no donation to our efforts is too small to help modernize and upgrade our facilities."

The man in our group said in a stage whisper, "I don't believe this. She has her hand out."

"It seems like a worthy cause to me," said one of the women who hadn't spoken up before. "Yes," her friend chimed in. "Where can we send a check to help?" Ms. Wexford distributed envelopes with an address where we could donate. Then she invited us to stand up and follow her into the technical department. The tour of the restoration lab was underwhelming. I'd guessed right earlier. The financial catastrophe had affected all areas of The Ringling, from maintaining the infrastructure to financing research equipment. I could see by Melanie's face that she thought so, too. This part of the tour took less than half an hour, and soon Ms. Wexford was saying cheerio to our group and thanking us for coming this afternoon.

"I need to run, Aunt Barbara," Melanie said to me as we headed back to the public foyer.

I was hoping for a cup of coffee and a gossipy girl talk session on our afternoon together. I tried to keep the disappointment off my face, but it must have shown since Melanie hugged me extra hard and promised to drop by the following day for a coffee and a chat. "It's just that I've got a date later this evening and need to go home and change."

I totally understood and told her I looked forward to hearing all about it in the morning. Before Melanie left, I stopped a guard and asked for directions to the ladies' room. "We'll be closing in fifteen minutes, ma'am," the security guard, a florid young man with a distinctive blonde pompadour, informed me. "Don't take too much time, please. We need to lock up on schedule."

"I'll be on my way, Aunt Barbara. Talk to you soon," Melanie said as she breezed through the plate-glass doors of the entrance.

I looked around and noticed I was one of the few remaining visitors in the foyer. "Now don't forget about me," I said to the security guard, who pointed me to the facilities around the corner.

"Don't worry, ma'am," the nice young man said reassuringly. "You have time. I'll check on you before I close up."

"Don't lock me in!" I joked.

Little did I know the joke was on me.

CHAPTER SEVEN

"A Night at The Ringling Museum"

The bathroom was old and could have used a remodel, but what the hey, The Ringling was broke. Now that I knew it, I could see the signs everywhere. Little square black and white tiles and slabs of gray-white marble, the dull, not highly polished kind, covered every surface. It looked so '70s. The sinks had rust marks where many years of dripping faucets had stained the porcelain. The floor tiles were chipped, and the trash can was overflowing with paper. There were four toilet stalls, and at least the toilets were new.

After washing my hands and reapplying my lipstick, I put my things back in my bag, took a last look in the mirror, and gave my hair a pat. I reached for the light switch as I was leaving when the light dimmed on its own. *Weird.*

Outside in the corridor, it was very quiet. The lights were dimmed like in the bathroom, though early evening light crept in through the foyer's glass doors. The ticket desk was deserted. No one was around. A metal gate, which I had never seen before, blocked the entry into the sculpture courtyard from the portico. *This is creepy.* Refusing to panic, I called out as loud as I could, "Hello, hello! Anybody there?"

Silence.

I called out again. Walking up to the glass exit doors, I pushed them one by one. They didn't budge. It was then that I noticed they were bolted tight. The place was locked up. *Oh my God! This isn't funny.*

I knocked on the glass. All I could see outside was the cracked cement stairway that led down to the drive with the big statue of a bull tossing a young damsel on its horns. The driveway was empty, and to the side, I could see my car. The only one left in the parking lot. *You'd think that would alert somebody!* I was pretty furious by now. *I told that guard I was going to the ladies' room,* I fumed. Then my anger broke, and I became scared. This was no joke.

"Help!" I yelled in earnest. Where was everybody? This couldn't be happening. I'd have to find the guard. Surely there must be a night watchman. My hollering wasn't getting me anywhere, so I decided to go find the night guard. I walked to the first big gallery with its Rubens' *The Triumph of the Eucharist over Idolatry* series. The walls were covered by five impressive paintings John Ringling had purchased from the Duke of Westminster in 1926. Despite the off-putting title, they were quite famous. I'd learned on prior guided tours of the museum that the other paintings from this series were in the Louvre.

Though the lighting was dim, I could see well enough. At first, the big colorful figures in the paintings made for cheery company. Since no guard seemed to be in the Rubens Gallery, I doubled back to the lobby and caught a glimpse of the Saint Clare painting as I turned around. This was a Spanish Princess,

Isabella Clara Eugenia of the Netherlands, Infanta of Spain, who Rubens had depicted as the sainted Clare wearing her nun's black habit. Now, her dark eyes seemed to drill into me, and I got spooked. I hurried back into the vestibule as if someone was chasing me. "Help! Somebody! Guard!"

I'd had enough and scrabbled in my purse for my cell phone. I'd call Sam, that's what I'd do. Then I remembered he was working the late shift at the factory tonight. No calls allowed. Okay, I'd call Melanie. She was on a date, but this was an emergency. Still, I hesitated a little. Why spoil a good time for her? I know! I'll call my good friend Jill, Jack's wife.

So, I called Jill, and it rang and rang until it rang out. I tried again and this time left a message. Shoot. I'd have to call Melanie after all. Another ring out and another embarrassed message, I couldn't believe it! My hour of need, and no one was answering their phone. I dialed Sam and left a sad little message about my predicament that he wouldn't pick up until after his shift. I knew I could count on my Prince Charming to come to my rescue as soon as he heard my plaintive distress call. How much overtime were they working tonight? *Come on! What was I doing wasting valuable time and battery life like this? I should just dial 911.* As I had that realization, the bars on my phone showed that I was out of power. I dropped my phone back into my bag, thoroughly disgusted with myself. What was I to do now? Keep looking for the guard, I suppose.

Oh! Maybe there's an intercom that connects through to The Ringling security office from reception. What a brilliant idea! I rushed over to the reception desk and found the semicircular counter was as bare as the shelf underneath it. All the drawers were locked. I stifled a sob. It was getting darker.

At least it isn't pitch dark. I counted my blessings. There were security lights on at intervals. I headed toward one of them on the other side of the foyer from the Rubens' room. When I entered, I saw the bulk of a big, tall, dark figure.

"Guard!" I called excitedly. "Can you help me? I got locked in the museum." To my surprise, the dark, bulging figure didn't turn around when I called out. Undaunted, I approached at a good clip, coming to a screeching halt in front of a giant statue of a naked woman balancing on her tiptoes. It was a voluptuous Gaston Lachaise statue, not a portly security guard. "This is awful! Where are the guards?" I said aloud to the voluptuous French lady.

I turned into a doorway to my left and found myself in a small gallery that I'd never seen before and was completely new to me; I thought I knew all the galleries. The old-fashioned mahogany and glass cases were filled with a collection of elaborately worked gold objects encrusted with jewels. Were they belts or diadems, ornaments for gods or rulers? The surrounding walls were hung with stone plaques covered with primitive writing, which looked part-Greek, part-cuneiform. *Hmm*, I thought. *They bore a faint resemblance to the stone object left at my house by my non-paying renter.* A big map showed arrows pointing to some places on the Arabian Peninsula with question marks. I made a mental note to check this room out further at some later date. *Who knew The Ringling had objects from the Middle East?*

I wandered on to where they kept the 19th and 20th century collections. In passing, I noted a favorite of mine, *Autumn Rain in the Woods* by Charles Burchfield. It was not grandiose like the Rubens on the other side of the hall, but it was somehow very interesting in its simplicity. It reminded me of New York City or Chicago, where most of Sarasota's inhabitants, including me, had originally come from. Next to it was a little Arthur Dove called *Mars, Red, Yellow and Green*. His paintings were very abstract and full of personal symbolism. This one showed a rainbow or a sunset. Next to the Arthur Dove was a gem of a small Degas. Two ballerinas were rehearsing their steps as seen from the orchestra pit. The pastel colors of the dancers' costumes and their pink skin contrasted with the unusual angle of Degas' *prise de vue* from behind the artificial glow of the footlights.

I had always wanted to touch a Degas with its luscious colors and texture, but of course, I never dared to do so. You weren't allowed to touch the artwork. It was forbidden, unthinkable behavior. I was tempted. I looked around. There was no guard in sight. Then it hit me like a bolt out of the blue. What better way to call attention to my plight than to set off the burglar alarm on a painting? That should bring someone running. Although it went against every fiber of my moral code, I went right up to the little canvas in its carved gilt frame and stroked it gently, expecting the buzz of an alarm any moment.

What a great idea, I applauded myself, except no alarm went off. Perplexed, I jiggled the elaborate gold frame a bit. Nothing. No warning buzzer. No sirens. No footsteps running toward me. Nothing at all. Now I really gave it the old college try and attempted to lift the painting off the wall. It was heavier than I expected, and it didn't budge. And no alarm went off, again. *How very strange.* I stood back and glared at the Degas, as if it had somehow betrayed me.

What the heck? The alarm system is on the fritz, too? The Ringling is clearly falling apart. After indulging in self-pity for a while, I decided to change my attitude. After all, things could be a lot worse. Since I seemed to be trapped for a while, I decided to make the best of my time alone here. It could be very special. I have a world-class art collection all to myself. I thought, *A night at The Ringling Museum!* It was just like a movie scenario. Boy, would I have a tale to tell over several dinners. And someone was bound to get my message soon and come running to save me.

With a new confidence, I made peace with the situation. I set off on my own to visit the galleries, all the while on the lookout for a guard along the way. I was *en route* to the Renaissance period, where I noticed a painting by Giuseppe Arcimboldo. He had a series of portraits, the faces composed of beautifully painted fruits and vegetables. It made me hungry. I would give anything to be home right now, making a salad as big as that man's head to accompany a gorgeous bread like one from *The Great British Baking Show* I liked to watch.

An escape to the next gallery didn't help with my munchies. This was 16th-century Netherlands with bounteous fruits, vegetables, shellfish, game, all the pleasures of the palate displayed in gorgeous still life. My mouth was watering. A beautiful exotic bird in the painting *Still Life With Parrots* by Jan Davidsz de Heem seemed to be inviting me to the banquet table. What a mouthful of a name, but that's what it said on the information card.

I reached the English 18th-century gallery. Here, Joshua Reynolds and Thomas Gainsborough's equestrian paintings of generals and lords of the British realm dominated. In the French gallery, I found the lords and ladies of Versailles disguised as shepherds and shepherdesses, frolicking on tree swings in luscious gardens.

I was musing about moments of history caught by the painters' brush when, with a start, I noticed a wall telephone by the doorway for the next gallery.

Holding my breath, I picked up the receiver and was so happy to hear a dial tone. But who to call? I tried zero for the operator. Then 911. Nothing happened. Frantically, I jiggled the switch hook, calling, "Hello, hello?" into the handpiece. There was no answer. It must have been for incoming calls only. Or maybe I needed a code to dial out? My hopes were dashed.

Somewhere, a clock chimed out nine o'clock. If the timepiece was correct, I had been locked in for four hours. I felt defeated and isolated. It didn't help that Marie Antoinette eyed me scornfully from underneath her fabulous hairdo. "Talk about having problems! Now she was in over her head, and then she lost hers completely." I shuddered and pressed on.

I decided I was becoming delirious with hunger, and to be honest, very, very tired. I pushed on through the Italian Renaissance, where I noticed the *La Sultana Rossa or Russa* by Titian, the same one Ms. Wexford had talked about in what now seemed like weeks ago, though it was only a few hours. A flash of light just beyond the French windows brought me to a sudden stop. There was the sound of an outboard motor revving in the distance. It rose to a crescendo and gradually died away. These windows looked onto the back courtyard of the museum, past the Renaissance sculpture gardens, toward Sarasota Bay. In the dark of the moonless night, I thought I saw brief flashes of light. Lightning? No, it wasn't high enough in the sky. The lights were more like flashlight beams. Maybe it was the guards patrolling the museum grounds? A feeling of hope coursed through me, but then the lights flickered, and I thought I must be imagining things.

Wait a minute! A shadow was outlined against a pink wall of the museum. Someone *was* out there! I banged on the windowpane as hard as I could. I jumped up and down, shouting at the top of my lungs for attention. "Help! Help!" I called out. "You there! Help me! Look over here! Here!" They didn't hear me. Whoever they were, out there at this time of night, they skulked about, keeping to the shadows.

I thought of breaking a windowpane, but what could I use? I found a ballpoint pen in my purse, which I pounded against the glass as hard as I could, getting nowhere. My keys were ineffective, as well. It was a good deal harder to break a window than I thought.

Outside, the lights disappeared, leaving me all alone again. I started to cry. I had done a good job so far of keeping my spirits up, but the charm of being locked in the museum was gone. Surely, someone should have gotten one of my phone messages by now. Surely, someone was missing me.

I slumped onto one of the silk upholstered benches with the "Please do not sit" placard and stretched out full length. Above me, the handsome ceiling decorations looked a million miles away. My sandals slipped off onto the floor, and I made myself as comfortable as I could on the narrow bench. I felt exhausted. I wondered what Sam was doing right now and if he had heard my message yet. I remembered that I was supposed to attend a meeting of the film festival committee the day after tomorrow. I made a mental note to myself that we were running low on coffee filters. I was compiling a grocery list in my mind when my eyelids flickered, once, twice ...

CHAPTER EIGHT

"Sarasota Dreamin'"

I dreamt. Of course, I dreamt. I always have the weirdest dreams when I'm stressed. And I always remember them in the minutest detail.

'*Lie down here,*' read the note above the bench, and so I lay down. Only the bench was now a striped swing decorated with beautiful silk tassels. The swing was strung between two tall trees with delicate foliage in a clearing of the Barbizon Forest in France. An attendant, a young Venetian blackamoor wearing a turban, rocked it rhythmically back and forth. Another created a gentle breeze with a giant fan of ostrich feathers. The gentle motion of both relaxed me. There was a fringed pillow supporting my head, which was very comfortable. I was suffused by a feeling of contentment.

How clever of me to have found this flowering bower where I could rest and restore myself in the company of French ladies in their exquisite taffeta gowns with lace bodices, and

English gentlemen wearing velvet breeches and shoes with diamond buckles. Their handsome steeds with saddles of tooled leather grazed nearby on the lush grass, watched over by proud-looking grooms in polished knee-high boots.

A Cheshire Cat was watching me. Actually, no, it wasn't a cat—it changed into a colorfully plumed parrot sitting on a golden stand next to his mistress. This regal lady was hand-feeding him tidbits of *petit four*. I felt hungry and I reached for a little cake for myself when the arrival of enormous red lobsters and giant pink crabs set the parrot screeching. The crustaceans scuttled through the forest glen, their beady eyes on long stalks sweeping this way and that. My aristocratic companions became upset and quickly melted away, leaving me alone, except for the parrot who shrieked, "Hello, Hello!" and took off into the air on enormous red, blue, and yellow wings.

In wonderment, I realized that I was riding on his back. We soared into the sky and flew over Italy. I could see the boot-like outline of the country from my perch above as he flew north toward Florence and then Venice. We hovered over the Grand Canal. I clutched at the bird's feathery neck, and he squawked, "Don't worry. I have experience with the King of England's collection at Windsor Castle. I will fly us home."

The parrot flew us out over the ocean, where ships with billowing sails passed modern ocean liners. I recognized the SS France, on which I once crossed the Atlantic. I strained to see my old cabin window when the parrot called out, "Ring, Ring. Who's there? Who's there?"

Should I answer? Was it one of those 'knock knock, who's there' jokes? I racked my brain for an answer. It was so important not to get it wrong. Then I had an inspiration: Ling, Ling," I replied.

"Ringling, Ringling," my parrot cawed the answer to the riddle happily in his eerily human way as he swooped toward the white crested ocean in a dizzying dive. I clung tight, afraid of the crashing waves. Suddenly, the sea turned into a perfectly calm, tropical lagoon with gorgeous turquoise water. We were in Florida!

The parrot's feathers became slippery like silk. My fingers lost their grip, and I slipped from his back, turning head over heels until I landed *splat* on a soft sandy beach. Miraculously, I was unhurt. I looked around me and felt so elated. I knew this place! It was Islamorada in the Florida Keys. I recognized the giant Norfolk pine at the Cheetah Lodge behind the local library. The thirty-foot tree was decorated with tinsel like it always was for Christmas. Even the tallest branches were decorated. The silver decorations swayed in the warm breeze off the ocean. *How did they get them up there*, I wondered?

Suddenly, I realized that I was wearing only a fur coat made of the skins of little animals like minks. Oh, no! I didn't have anything on underneath! Not even a bathing suit! I ran toward the hotel entrance, trying to keep the coat pulled together, but it kept flapping open. People were strolling around the reception area, and I stopped and hid behind a Bird of Paradise potted palm on the walkway by the hotel. I was so ashamed. *Would I be discovered?* I crouch-walked to hide behind the next potted plant, slowly making my way toward the door, always on the lookout for prying eyes. *How had I gotten myself into this awkward situation? Why was I always taking foolish risks?*

Sam was standing by the hotel entrance. He was smiling. Was he waiting for me? Sam would understand. I ran toward him, but he kept receding farther and farther away. Always out of reach. "Sam, Sam," I called, but he couldn't hear me. Then the earthquake started. The ground around me heaved and shook. My whole body rocked—

"Lady. Hey, lady. Get up. You can't be here. What do you think you're doing?"

I opened my eyes with a start. A guard in a brown uniform

was shaking me by the shoulder. I was confused, and it took me a moment to remember where I was. *Oh, yeah! The bench in the Astor room of The Ringling Museum.* I snapped out of my drowsiness.

"Mister, am I happy to see you!" I cried. "I've been locked in here since closing time. I was looking for you everywhere. Where have you been? I called, I telephoned, I banged on the window. I even tried to set off the burglar alarm. Nothing happened! You gotta help me get outta here." I quickly rose to my feet.

The guard stepped back, his face unsmiling. "Not so fast. What have you been up to? I'm taking you to the management office."

"What time is it?" I noticed the dimmer lights were off, and early morning sunlight poured through the windows.

"Follow me, please." The guard gripped my elbow a little too tightly to be comfortable.

"Let go of me. Don't touch me." I yanked my arm away.

"This way."

"*I'm* the one who's been wronged here!" I started to lose my temper. "Just give me a minute for a pit stop, and I'll follow you wherever you like. I told the guard last night that I was going to the powder room and to wait for me. Instead, I was locked in here all night. If anything, *I'm* the one owed an apology!"

He snorted rudely. "Look, lady, people were on duty all night, and I don't know what you're talking about."

By now, we'd passed through the Italian Renaissance and were back in the foyer. We were heading toward doors marked "Staff Only" when the main door flew open. Sam swept in with Melanie hot on his heels. I thought my knees would buckle with relief.

"What's going on here?" Sam thundered.

"This guy is trying to railroad me," I cried. "He's blaming me for the predicament the museum put me in."

"Are you all right, sweetie pie?" Sam wrapped an arm around me, all love and concern, and I felt tears prick my eyes, but didn't want to snivel in front of that bully of a guard.

Instead, I faced him full on, shoulders squared, and said, "I believe you were taking me to see the manager. Please lead the way. I wish to lodge a complaint against the museum." Melanie gave me a thumbs-up sign and a big smile of encouragement. We set out toward the "Staff Only" door.

The guard dutifully knocked on it. Sam and Melanie had come to my rescue, and this guy, whoever he was, was going to get an earful about the state of his security system.

CHAPTER NINE

"Ladies and Gentlemen, Welcome to the Big Top"

The three of us marched into the office of the security director, who had clearly just arrived for the morning and was looking over last night's record books. The guard said, "Good morning, Boss. I was doing my morning rounds, and I found this woman asleep in the Astor Room. She says she was locked in the museum all night. Next thing I know, these two friends of hers burst in to take her home."

"Thank you, Mike," the head honcho said to our escort. "I'll take it from here. You can get back to the Astor Room."

Without further ado, I sat down in the chair in front of the security director's desk and started to tell him my sad tale of woe. Sam and Melanie were standing behind me. "You incompetent boobies had me trapped in your museum since 6:00 p.m. yesterday. I called and shouted. I tried to set off the security alarms. I pounded on the windows. No one came to help me all night. What kind of an operation are you running here?"

"Madam, slow down, please. What are you yelling about? Let's start at the beginning," said the director of security, whose name was Elroy McBride, according to the plaque on his desk. If I had been expecting a big brute of a man, the head of security was just the opposite, a slender reed of a fellow with metal-rimmed glasses. His lips formed a smile, but his eyes studied me coldly. He asked me to state my name and explain what I had been doing here at The Ringling yesterday afternoon.

"I'm Barbara Waldheim. You can check your records to verify that my niece, Melanie, who is the young woman right behind me, and I were attending The Ringling's "Behind the Scenes" seminar on art restoration yesterday afternoon. When it ended about 5:45 p.m., I went to the bathroom and was locked in the museum, even though I put a guard on notice that I was going there, and he swore on a stack of Bibles that he wouldn't leave me stranded like he did."

"Really, Ms. Waldheim? That sounds unlikely. It sounds to me more as if you were hiding in the ladies' room waiting to sneak into the museum after hours," said the security director in a knowing, superior tone. "For what reason, I can only speculate, but probably not for any good reason."

"Now just a minute here, Mister," said Sam, getting offended on my behalf. "Are you implying that Barbara is lying? You'd better not be, or you'll have me to answer to."

"And just who are you, sir?" said McBride disdainfully, taking in Sam's work clothes and the faint whiff of hydraulic oil emanating from them.

The two men faced off threateningly when Melanie spoke up. "Aunt Barbara, isn't that photo on the wall behind Mr.

McBride's desk the same guard who promised to keep the museum open until you finished in the bathroom last night?"

"Why, Melanie, that's right." I shot her a grateful look. On the wall behind Elroy McBride's desk was a photo of the security guard of the month. He was the same guard we talked to yesterday evening. I pointed to it, telling the security director, "That's the guard who promised to wait for me to finish in the ladies' room before locking up last night. Let's call him in here, and he'll tell you what happened. I recognize his hairdo. He has a pompadour like Elvis, only blonde."

"Yes," Melanie said. "He can vouch for Aunt Barbara. I met him too before I left the building."

Elroy McBride hesitated not even a millisecond before informing us authoritatively that the security guard in question was not on duty today. McBride surely had an impressive memory for his underlings' days off.

I said, "Mr. McBride, we are wasting our time on minor details. In my opinion, it is much more important that I couldn't find a night watchman at The Ringling all last night. Where were the guards? That is the big question. I wandered around the galleries for hours looking for someone to help me. No one was on duty, and the alarm system was disabled. How do you explain that?"

To my surprise, the security director wasn't even interested in this startling information. He referred to the papers open on his desk for a few moments before saying, "Mrs. Waldheim, you are mistaken. The logs and record books from last night simply do not bear out your experience. I don't wish to impugn your integrity, but many times, people are subject to flights of fancy. In a stressful situation such as the one in which you found yourself, the mind plays tricks on a susceptible person. It is perfectly understandable," he said, his voice now dripping with simulated concern, his eyes assessing how his presentation was going over. "We are a public institution and must accept all kinds of visitors at the museum, and of course, we are used to treating them gently for their own well-being, no matter their age, physical or mental circumstances, or point of view."

The mealy-mouthed little bureaucrat paused a moment to allow the scope of his insinuation to sink in. Was he saying that I didn't have all my marbles? He continued, "If anything, it is the museum that is forced to be leery of your actions and unauthorized presence here last night." McBride's eyes gleamed unpleasantly, and a mean smile played around his lips. "I'm afraid I'll have to call the police. The Ringling can't take any chances."

Sam spoke up and said hotly, "Yes, you can certainly call the police, but if you do, first we'll have to call our lawyer."

The atmosphere in the little security office got extremely tense. Melanie, Sam, and I looked at each other with dismay. McBride twiddled his fingers on his desk, looking not entirely displeased at the effect his words had wrought.

"Check your security cameras," I demanded. "You will see that I was unceremoniously locked in, and there was no ill intent."

McBride squirmed.

An uncomfortable silence fell on the room.

Sam piped up, "That's a great idea. That way, we can put this whole thing to rest."

McBride stammered, "Unfortunately, the cameras are out of service at present. Our system is being upgraded."

How convenient, I thought to myself. Then I remembered something. "You know, Mr. McBride, just before I fell asleep on the bench, I saw lights outside at the rear of the building and what seemed to be someone or several people moving around with lights. Guardians, checking the perimeter? I tried to get their attention, but once again, I failed. I even thought I heard the noise of a motor, like the gunning of a speedboat. What was that all about? Another figment of my overactive imagination?"

At this, the security director blinked a few times behind his glasses, and his attitude underwent a sea change. It was as if the cast, the set, and the scenery were the same, but the script had been rewritten. Elroy McBride suddenly became terribly obliging and solicitous.

"Ms. Waldheim," he said. "You had a terrible experience. What was your niece's name? Melanie? Please sit down, Melanie. And you, sir," he said to Sam, "take a seat," indicating some chairs against the wall. He picked up the telephone receiver on his desk. "Let me order some coffee and Danish to be sent over from the Banyan Café on the museum grounds. It won't take but a minute. We can have breakfast together and continue our chat. I'm sure we can get this sorted out without further acrimony and without involving the police." McBride's eyes glittered with false bonhomie.

I didn't know about the others, but I felt relief and whiplash at the same time. The whole turnabout in his attitude was as phony as a counterfeit painting. "Thank you, Mr. McBride," I said. "I am hungry, but I'd like to go home and relax and forget all about this awful experience. What do you think, Sam and Melanie? Shall we be on our way?"

We all headed for the door. Before we left, McBride apologized for the unfortunate incident and pressed two free entrance passes to the museum and Cà d'Zan, the Ringling mansion, on each of us.

Melanie, Sam, and I walked down the cement stairs past the statue of the god Zeus disguised as a bull, tossing the maiden, Io, on its horns. I must admit I identified with her. I felt that I had been toyed with. To put it less politely, I had been "futzed" over.

However, at the present moment, as I breathed a sigh of relief that my ordeal was over, it felt great to be outside in the caressing air of the cool, sunny morning. The three of us headed across the walk to the parking lot to retrieve our respective vehicles. Standing by our cars, Sam and I gave each other a long hug.

"You really saved my bacon, Sam. You and Melanie arrived just in time. Thanks for the support."

"Don't mention it, my sweetie pie," Sam said, stroking my cheek. "There is something very rotten going on in that security department. I only wish I could have been more help."

"You two were great. You really backed up my story," I told him and my niece. Sam was headed back to work. He was doing two shifts back-to-back. Melanie had time before her first class to follow me back to the house on her motorcycle for a coffee.

"Goodbye, Sam. Have a good day. Call me later."

"Ok. Love you. See you tonight. Bye, Melanie."

"Bye, Sam. Let's get out of here," Melanie spoke for all of us.

———

Once back at my little Spanish-style hacienda, Melanie and I sat at the kitchen counter drinking steaming hot coffee out of brightly decorated glazed mugs, souvenirs from a trip to Santa Fe, New Mexico, and downing one mini-Entenmann's pastry after another. I ate all the apricot and she took all the raspberry. No wonder we got along so well.

"I'm feeling more and more like myself every minute. The whole experience is beginning to seem almost comical," I said.

"Perhaps, but Aunt Barbara, did you see Mr. McBride's reaction when you mentioned seeing lights and hearing a boat last night? You sure touched upon a sensitive area. Why, the guy shut down and then lit up like a faulty circuit."

"I know, Melanie. I could swear I heard a motor and saw flashlights at the rear of the museum. I'm sure I didn't make that up. What could have been going on last night? Why was no one on duty? And no footage from the security cameras? That just isn't credible. It's so mysterious." We both got quiet for several moments, thinking.

"Let's take our mugs of coffee out onto the back patio. I feel like I've been cooped up inside for too long. I need some air."

"Sure thing, Aunt Barbara."

The two of us moved onto the stone patio to sit under the bottlebrush tree, where I had positioned some rattan chairs. As we settled in, Melanie noticed the gas grill Sam had won at the company picnic. He and I had positioned it there on the patio at the ready. "Nice," she said. "A cook like Sam deserves a grill like that one."

"Sam wants to have a big barbecue soon to put it through its paces. You and Vroom Vroom will be invited, of course."

"We'll be happy to come." Melanie's attention was drawn to the carved rock leaning against the front leg of the grill. "What's that funny stone object? Is it from Home Goods?"

"Oh, that old thing. My deadbeat renter, Waylan, left it here. It's really his, I suppose. I don't know where he got it from exactly. We are going to use it under the left front leg to level off the grill, which wobbles here on the grass where the patio stones are cracking up. Melanie got up to take a closer look at the rock. "I think this looks like some kind of inscription. The writing looks interesting to me."

"Yeah, maybe? It's interesting in a rough-around-the-edges

way like its owner, Waylan Cooper. He's kind of a sore point with me. Let's change the subject."

"What was it like having the museum all to yourself, Aunt Barbara?"

"It was kind of cool. I touched a Degas. I mean, I stroked the canvas when I was trying to set off the alarm system."

"Wow! Really!"

"Uh-huh, and I danced around in the Boucher and Fragonard room. I curtsied to Marie Antoinette. I gave the finger to Isabella, the Infanta of Spain, because her eyes were scaring me. To tell you the truth, I'd rather visit a museum during regular hours. The lighting is a lot better. As long as it's not too crowded, the company of other visitors probably adds rather than detracts from the experience. Being all alone is mournful."

"I see what you mean. You can also take a guided visit, which adds to your enjoyment and knowledge. Speaking of adding to knowledge, I'd better get to class. And then I'm meeting Caterina, the woman on my film festival committee. She is turning out to be such a great friend. I really enjoy her company. What are you up to today? I hope you can relax."

"Yes. That's my plan. I'm going to start with a soak in the bathtub and move on to even less strenuous activities from there."

"Good for you, Aunt Barbara. I'll let you get on with it."

"Say, I forgot to ask you, what were you and Vroom Vroom up to last night while I was museum-going?"

"We were at this new club in Ybor City. It was wild. The band was fantastic. It was so loud and so crowded. That's why I didn't hear your messages until later."

"Well, better late than never, and all's well that ends well, and a few other old chestnuts which apply. Have a good day."

I escorted Melanie the short distance to the door, and we

stood under the overhang with the orchids where she pecked me on the cheek. "Take it easy today, Aunt Barbara." She opened the wrought iron gate of the courtyard and hesitated before closing it behind her again.

"Wait a minute," Melanie said, backtracking. "On second thought, I think I'll take a few photos of that stone carving with my cellphone to show to Caterina. She's looking for inspiration for new abstract scarf designs, and as long as I'm at it, I might like to run the photos by one of my art history professors." A moment later, she called out a goodbye, and I heard the roar of her bike as she sped off to school.

Back inside the house, I was just putting the coffee mugs and dishes in the sink when the telephone rang. I saw by the number that it was Jill. Well, it was about time she checked in with me. I couldn't wait to talk to her.

"Jill, where have you been? I just got home an hour ago. I spent the night locked in The Ringling Museum. They accused me of sneaking in. There were no guards on duty, no alarms working. You wouldn't believe the whole chain of events."

Jill was suitably surprised and indignant on my behalf. She said she'd fill Jack in on these amazing accusations, but her voice didn't have its usual verve.

"Are you OK? You don't sound quite like yourself today," I said to her. "I'm the one who just had the awful experience."

Jill chuckled ruefully and explained she'd been having her own problems. She and Jack had gotten into a huge fight over unpaid bills and his mother's bingo mania, and his sister's craziness. What a family she had to deal with! Marital hostilities had escalated to a fever pitch before calming down to a dull roar this morning. She sounded about as fed up and discouraged as I'd ever heard her.

"Barbara," Jill said, "let's get together later and talk all this through. I'm not working this afternoon. I was wondering if you want company when you go downtown to meet Waylan at the courthouse later today. I could go along with you."

Oops! I had completely forgotten about my court date with all the excitement. That's right. This afternoon, Waylan and I were scheduled to appear to give evidence before the judge in the matter of the unpaid rent and damages he owed me.

"Jill," I said into the phone, "would you believe that after last night, the date of the hearing had completely slipped my mind?"

So the two of us agreed that I'd pick her up in my car in two hours. That way, we would have plenty of time to park and get ourselves to where I needed to be for the hearing. We'd also have time to talk things over with one another.

Well, I thought to myself, *there goes my relaxing morning. It never rains, but it pours, to coin a phrase.*

CHAPTER TEN

"Twelve Steps and a Stubbed Toe"

I took a quick shower instead of that bubble bath I was dreaming of and got dressed for my court date with my deadbeat renter. I phoned Sam and left him a message about my court appearance with Waylan. I would brief him on the outcome when I saw him later that evening for our movie date at the Dollar Cinema, to be followed by dinner at the English Pub. There were a lot of Brits in Sarasota, and the pub was a popular casual eatery and bar serving endless glasses of Guinness stout with their foamy heads decorated by a shamrock that the barmaids knew how to design right in the froth on top.

I quickly got together the papers I needed to show the judge for the hearing. I got in the car and drove over to Jill's house off of Bee Ridge Road. No sooner did she get in the car than she started talking. If I thought she wanted to hear about my night locked in the museum, I was mistaken.

"Oh, Barbara! I don't like to bother you, but he's driving me crazy. I don't know if I can take it much longer. Between his mother and his crazy sister, I don't get any attention. Mother Gilbert goes to play bingo every afternoon at The Pines and then forgets how to come home on the bus. I have to go get her. Jack's sister, Liza, is forty-five years old and still boy crazy. There is always another drama about her latest love affair."

"Hmmm," I murmured sympathetically. "It's that bad, huh?"

"Jack is the most infuriating man! He drives me up the wall!" she huffed, "He'll never change! He's always rattling around the house, making a mess, drinking another beer. He's forever on the computer. He's obsessed. We're always overspending. We never have any money."

I knew all about Jill and Jack's problems. Once Jill had moved in with me for a while to get away from him. Another time, we had looked around for an apartment she could rent to use as a stepping stone to leaving her husband for good. Each time, she had ended up getting back together with him. He was the magnet, and she was like the metal filings.

With all this in the back of my mind, I said, "How's it going with your job at Jared's Tile House? Are you still putting in some hours there?"

Perking up slightly, Jill answered, "Yes, I sure am. Jared is fun to work with, and he appreciates my design ability. The pay helps out with our finances, but Jack is always incurring more expenses, so we never catch up."

"What about the investigation for the ICE people? How's that going?"

Jill admitted that there might be some good news on that front. Jack had hit pay dirt connecting cell phone numbers dialed by his Middle Eastern tile workers to the cell phone number of a known terrorist sympathizer in Tampa. A bigger fish. That man is the Al Kader Bill mentioned to you. The one who owned a big chain of Subway restaurants in the Tampa Bay area. The one Jack suspected of involvement in a complicated scheme to finance terrorist activity by exporting expensive stolen cars. Jack's next assignment was to follow this money trail.

I didn't really understand the ins and outs of my friend's explanation of this scheme, but the salient point was that ICE, the U.S. federal anti-terrorist agency, was very interested in Jack's information. Jack and Jill were both excited by the prospect of the reward money dangled by the ICE people.

"Sounds good to me. That will be something to look forward to," Jill said, "if it ever pans out. Oh, by the way, I almost forgot to tell you something about the shenanigans going on at The Ringling Museum."

"Really, what do you know?"

"Well, after our call, I told Jack that you said there was no working security last night in the museum galleries, and he said that it might be a coincidence, but that some of the phone calls he's been tracing have been numbers attributed to The Ringling Museum. He was perplexed. He thought it was probably a fluke or a mistake."

I said, getting excited, "Are you thinking what I'm thinking? Could there be some link? After all, there is a gross discrepancy between my experience that the museum was left unguarded last night and the security chief's assessment that all systems were up and running.

"Did I tell you that I saw someone with a light at the rear of the museum by the Bay and heard a motorboat in the middle of the night?"

"What!" Jill exploded. "We've got to tell Jack about that." She was immediately all in sync and cooperating with her husband and partner again. From experience, I had learned not to say anything too negative about Jack, which could be held against me when they got back together. "I think you need to take this to the police," she advised.

"The head of The Ringling security department was threatening me with just that, to call the police on me, until I told him about the mysterious lights and noises in the courtyard. Then he couldn't get rid of me fast enough."

"They treated you very shabbily. At the very least, they owe you an explanation," Jill opined.

"I agree with you. I can't let them ride roughshod over me like this. But I'm reluctant to go to the police. What am I going to say? I have no proof. And I can't justify my presence in the museum after hours if they start pointing fingers."

By this time, Jill and I had parked the car, found the court building, gone through the metal detector, and were sitting on a bench talking in the waiting area of the Sarasota courthouse.

At two o'clock, my case was called to the docket. As a court officer led me into the judge's chamber, Jill waved to me for luck. If I could get at least some restitution for the damage Waylan had caused, I would feel a lot better and less gullible.

It took only a minute for the judge to see that Waylan had not shown up for the hearing, so she found in favor of the plaintiff—me. It was anticlimactic. I didn't even have to recount my story or show my bills.

Next, I was directed over to the clerk of the court's office to file the paperwork. "Ah, well," I laughed, chalking it up to experience. "We told you this might happen," Jill reminded me, "but at least there is now a record of your damages on file." We headed for the multilevel garage where I had parked. As we exited the elevator, who should appear in front of us but the defendant, Mr. Waylan Cooper himself, hair slicked back, cowboy boots on his feet, neckerchief tied around his throat, and fancy Stetson hat in his hand. He certainly was a nice-looking deadbeat. He was Hollywood handsome: tall and slim with broad shoulders, chiseled features, and that thousand-kilowatt smile. When he turned it on, it was hard to resist.

"Howdy, Barbara," he purred at me, looking abashed as he twiddled the brim of his cowboy hat in his hands. "Howdy, ma'am," he said to Jill. "I hope I didn't startle y'all there."

"Well, as I live and breathe, if it isn't the elusive Waylan Cooper himself, too little, too late," I greeted him snarkily. "We were waiting for you back there at the courthouse, me and the judge and the court clerk."

"Okay, Barbara, listen here for a minute," the fellow wheedled. "I know I owe you an apology."

"Hah! An apology? You owe me more than that. Here's the paperwork." I waved the documents in his direction. "You owe me $1,500 according to the City of Sarasota Small Claims Court."

I wasn't sure where I was getting the courage to talk to him like this, but I was fearless for the moment, and it felt very good.

Waylan bobbed his head up and down and said, "I get it. I understand where you're coming from, and I'd love to pay you."

His admission stopped me in my tracks for a moment. He smiled his engaging smile at me and then continued, "There's just one little problem ... I'm broke, flat broke." He chuckled a bit to himself as if amused or embarrassed at this teeny difficulty.

"Oh, I see, you find this whole thing funny," I said. "Let me introduce you to my friend here. This is Jill Gilbert. You may remember her husband, Jack Gilbert. He is the man who served you with notice to vacate my house, where you were freeloading. Jack and Jill don't take guff from riff-raff like you.

So don't waste her time." I started to move off toward my car with Jill.

"Hold on there, little lady. Not so fast," Waylan pleaded. "I want to make you some restitution. Let me explain."

"Make it fast," I said. I'll give you two minutes, and then I'll be on my way. I've wasted enough time on the likes of you."

"I read you loud and clear, boss lady," Waylan said respectfully. "Listen now," he hesitated and then affirmed, "I'm cleaning up my act. No more booze. No more pot. No more scams. I'm in a twelve-step program, and I want to make amends to you. It's part of my recovery."

I looked Waylan hard in the eyes. He looked back at me, and to my surprise, he held my gaze. He seemed sincere. If this was a snow job, he was even more talented than I already gave him credit for.

Waylan continued, "I've got a new girlfriend. Her name is Shelley Dupree. She's a grown woman, not a no-account. She's a real good influence on me. She's a bank officer. I'm not kidding you. That's her job. She's got me on the straight and narrow path, and I'm feeling better than I have since my Army days. So, I repeat, I can't pay you what I owe, but tell you what, you keep that stone I found in Sarasota Bay with the writing on it. It might be worth a little something. I want you to have it. And here's a coupla bucks—he pressed some money into my hand. I'll pay you more when I can."

"Okay, I wish you luck with your recovery. I hope you turn over a new leaf," I told Waylan as Jill and I walked to my car. Waylan's avowal had taken the wind out of my sails. I felt there was no point in further recriminations.

As Jill and I got in my car, Waylan even opened the door for me.

We were putting on our seat belts when Jill asked me what Waylan meant about a stone carving.

I explained that he left a stone object behind at my house, like a broken tile with symbols on it. I was just about to start the engine when Jill put her hand on my arm to stop me and said, "Wait a minute, Barbara. Did Waylan say he found that stone in Sarasota Bay? That is bizarre. I want to ask him about that."

I put down my window and called out to Waylan, who was just heading for the stairs to exit the parking lot.

Waylan walked back to my little green sports car and bent down to talk to us through the open window.

"Where did you say you found that stone carving, young man?" Jill was ready to give Waylan the 3rd degree.

"I was out on my boat fishing for grouper around the sandbar off Lido Key a couple of months back when I found it. It happened when I was living at Barbara's place. I jumped in the water to untangle a line when I stubbed my toe on that piece of stone in the shallow water. I damn near broke my big toe on that baby!" Waylan told us, reliving his discovery.

"Really?" Jill said skeptically.

"When I looked at it, the symbols reminded me of some of the markings on the ancient ruins I saw when I served in Fallujah province in Iraq."

"Is that so? You served in Iraq?" Jill questioned. She seemed surprised. "My husband was there, too."

"Well, how about that! We're brothers in arms," Waylan said companionably.

"I didn't think you'd be interested in ancient art, Waylan," I said. "You're full of surprises today."

"Yes, ma'am, those old temples and some of the protective walls were still standing near my Army base in Anbar province. I was kind of a history buff back in high school. The ruins were pretty cool and our unit tried to look out for 'em, but with a war going on and all ... then, too, their leaders don't really care if they get destroyed because they predate Islam ..."

"Well, have a nice day, Waylan, good luck in recovery." I cut Waylan off short. I wasn't interested in hearing a lecture from him.

I drove off down the ramp to the garage exit as Waylan gave a couple of waves after us with his hat.

"Will wonders never cease?" Jill said with a low whistle. I don't know what to make of that guy. A new start? He served in the Persian Gulf? Imagine! He tripped on a stone carving in Sarasota Bay? What are the chances of that? Did you know he found that carving in the bay?"

"No, I had no idea. That sounds like a tall tale even for Waylan," I said, chuckling. "I don't really like the object. It's a dull color and very rough at the edges, like Waylan. It doesn't go with my Mexican decor. It's like a broken piece of something. My niece Melanie thought it looked interesting, and come to think of it, I saw some similar objects on a wall in one of The Ringling galleries. I was actually surprised, since it's a collection of Renaissance art."

Jill mused, "That's intriguing. Wouldn't it be funny if there were a connection? The museum is just up the coast from Lido Key."

We both laughed.

Jill seemed a bit less stressed after our afternoon out, having unburdened herself about her problems with her husband. She was now eager to tell Jack about our encounter with Army veteran Waylan Cooper, and his claim that he'd found a carved piece of stone in Sarasota Bay. We gave each other a little hug across the gear shift console, and Jill got out of the car. I watched her walk to her front door and go inside.

I continued on to Whitney Plaza to meet Sam for the senior movie showing at the Dollar Cinema. The hydraulic valve plant where he worked was just down the highway from the theater. After the early show, we went out to dinner at the British Pub in the mall. Over fish and chips, I recounted how Waylan was a no-show at court but showed up at the parking garage, where he swore he was a new and improved version of himself by virtue of a new girlfriend and a twelve-step program.

"He promised to make amends to us when he earns enough money. For now, he gave me twenty dollars and officially gifted us the stone carving he left at the house, which, listen to this," I told my boyfriend between bites of cod, "Waylan says he found in the shallow water off Lido Key. He stubbed his toe on it one day when he was out fishing on the sandbar there.

Sam mulled over this new bit of information. "He found it in the bay of all places? That's incredible," Sam said. "So, to make a long story short, we now have exclusive bragging rights to Waylan's marine trash, slash, flotsam, and jetsam."

"Correct. Yes, it's ours for good. You know, Melanie thinks that carving is more than some kind of oddity or tourist souvenir, and Waylan thinks it might have some value, too. I'm beginning to think my ability to evaluate its quality was clouded by the way I received it. I think I never could appreciate it properly because of the way it was dumped at my house.

"Maybe we should bring that stone in from the patio and display it in the house somewhere," I said.

"Yes, but it works so well as a support under the leg of the gas grill," Sam replied. "It doesn't seem to hurt it."

"Sam, did I tell you about that room of ancient objects from Arabia that I saw in The Ringling while I was locked in? I'm going to do some research into those antiquities. I didn't know The Ringling had any collection like that. I'd like to learn about it."

"Sure, that's a great idea," Sam enthused, agreeable as

usual. "Then you can tell me what you learn and we'll both know."

"Well, Sam, I never! Talk about a second-hand, piggyback method to acquire knowledge," I said huffily, partly teasing. "I'd never reveal my hard-earned research to such a do-nothing slug!"

"Now you're calling me a lazy do-nothing!" Sam said, pretending to take offense. "And I'm the one who works so hard, putting in all these hours at the hydraulics plant! Well, no matter, I have my ways of worming information out of you, my lovely— irresistible methods you can't resist."

He took the fork from my hand and put it down on the table. Luckily, I had finished my dinner. Then he gently took my hand, turned it over, and started covering the inside of my arm with little kisses, working his way up from my wrist toward my elbow. It tickled a little and felt good at the same time. It was embarrassing in the restaurant. "Stop it, Sam," I said, looking around and blushing.

"Like I told you," he intoned ominously, "the torture is just beginning."

I caught on to Sam's flirtatious mood and whispered in mock fright, "Ooh, la, la, please don't hurt me. I'll tell you everything you want to know, but not here." We quickly finished up our meal and paid for it, partly with the windfall from Waylan. Then we hurried home.

CHAPTER ELEVEN

Life got busy after my ordeal at The Ringling. Somehow, I never did get around to looking into those Arabian antiquities that had intrigued me. In fact, I kind of avoided thinking about The Ringling after my unpleasant experience there. I was surprised that the museum didn't contact me to apologize or something. I was offended by the way they had treated me.

But more to the point, I was kept quite busy with other activities. I had a full schedule of classes and workshops in painting and printmaking at the Sarasota Art Center. I continued to volunteer at the Orchid Research Center over at Selby Gardens, and my friend, Summer, and our wider group of friends met twice a week for yoga class followed by lunch at one of the places on Pineapple Avenue. I was also recruited by Melanie to help with the installation of her latest photo project exhibition at her school. It was part of her degree program, and she had a lot riding on showcasing her latest work so that her professors would support a grant proposal she was writing. She was hoping to get sponsored to spend the next academic year doing research at Villa I Tati near Florence, Italy, a part of Columbia University dedicated to research in the Arts.

On weekends, Sam and I took full advantage of the ballets, operas, and theater companies' programs in the city. Sarasota offered a smorgasbord of cultural activities. My Sarasota Film Festival Committee met punctually every week, and I tried to attend most meetings. Our organizational work had started to bear fruit.

The months were passing, and preparations for the celebrity luncheon party for film festival donors in early February, organized by Melanie and Caterina's committee, were on track. The drawing card of their luncheon was an actress whose feature film was in competition at the festival, Alicia Silverstone. She was very interested in animal rights and would be promoting her work as an animal rights activist at their luncheon. Spaces were at a premium, and a few lucky festival volunteers, including Melanie and Caterina Alvarez, were also invited to attend. The two young women had become very friendly in the course of working together.

My subcommittee, whose job was organizing the party for the best foreign film announcement, was also making progress. The schedule of foreign films to be screened had been published along with their venues, some at the historic Burns Court Cinema, some at the Regal Multiplex Theatres. Our early evening event would feature casual, catered food and drink and would be open to the public for a modest entry ticket price. At the end of the party, a movie star whose name was still a "secret"—in other words, Peter and Marybelle were still trying to call in a favor to snare a big name—would announce the People's Choice of the Best Foreign Film Entry of the Year.

———

November quickly turned to December and the holidays were now upon us. Vroom Vroom was invited to spend them with Melanie and my sister Amy's family in Philadelphia. We were unable to join them since Sam's vacation time was maxed out during our long summer holiday in France. Sam and I drove the young couple to the airport, all excited. Sarasota's airport was a pleasure because it was so petite compared to those in bigger cities. We waved them off, watching as they disappeared into the security area, holding their winter coats on their arms.

Meanwhile, our calendar was filling up with holiday party invitations, beginning with Sam's annual company Christmas party at the Classic Car Museum. That night, everyone was talking in whispers about the office romance, which had reached a crisis stage. It was common knowledge that company president Charlie Stutz's wife, Marilyn, had found out about his dalliance with the front office secretary. The big question was what was going to happen next. *Would Mrs. Stutz file for divorce?* She was the big attraction of the party, with everyone watching how she would treat Charlie. Would they dance together? How would she treat Nancy, her rival, the other woman? Would they wish each other a happy holiday? The unfolding drama had employees concerned about the stability of the company, creating an underlying anxiety among the partygoers.

At one point, the evening's tension resulted in a fist fight over a torn sports jacket. One of the guys had borrowed it from his coworker but failed to take good care of it. Even the cars on display seemed lackluster. But it was a chance to dress up and for Sam to show his allegiance to the company. We left the party earlier than we expected, around 9:00.

When we returned home, I asked Sam to park in the little circular driveway in front of my house instead of the side drive. I wanted to see how the new vines I had planted were doing, where I was training them to climb on the front wall. It was a beautiful, clear night. I had left the pretty Spanish-style wrought iron lights burning on either side of the entrance gate into the courtyard, in the center of which sat a little fountain in front of the main door. My hacienda was so cute as long as you didn't inspect it too carefully, or you would notice the flaws in wrought iron work and the places where the stucco was chipped. As Sam and I lingered to embrace before entering the courtyard, I chanced to look down at the flower bed near the gate, and saw a jeweled necklace lying in the sandy soil. It was a beautiful string of delicate red, yellow, and black beads glittering softly in the gatepost light.

"Look at that!" I said to Sam, pointing at the slender strand about five inches long, shimmering in the sand. As I reached down to touch it, Sam grabbed my hand.

"Wait a moment, sweetie pie," my ever-vigilant protector said. "I think that's a snake, not a piece of jewelry. It might even be one of the most poisonous varieties they have here in Florida, the Eastern coral snake."

"That pretty little thing!" I gasped, trembling, pulling back my hand and sheltering my body against Sam's. Then I thought to myself that Sam was joking, and I said to him, "Oh, you devil! You're kidding me! You can have a cuddle anytime. You don't have to tease me."

"Honestly, I'm serious," Sam continued. "Let's look more closely. Is the creature red, yellow, and black or yellow, red, and black? *Red next to black is safe for Jack. Red next to yellow will kill any fellow.* That's the saying I learned when I was doing landscaping work."

"What!" I exclaimed, mystified. "I can't tell. You're talking in riddles."

"I am talking about the difference in coloration between the Eastern coral snake, which is highly venomous and related to the cobra, and the Scarlet king snake, which is non-venomous. The way to tell them apart is by the distribution of their colorful markings, which are the same but in a different order."

But before we could consider our little critter further, the colorful little string of beads had vanished from sight.

"Oh, Sam! It was beautiful and delicate, but a snake! At my garden gate! It's too much wildlife for me. It gives me the willies!"

My partner gave a nervous laugh and told me that it would be alright. "Those reptiles are very shy," he said unconvincingly.

Suddenly, with a bang and a whoosh, a fancy sedan came shooting out of our side driveway. "What the Bejesus!" I gasped. We didn't know which end was up! The snake! The bang! The car! What was going on? Who was in our driveway?

Why hadn't the neighbors' dogs barked a warning that someone was present? Those two pitbulls, Duke and his daughter, Dukette, barked their heads off at Sam and me without fail whenever we parked in the side drive. And they knew us, more or less. Where were they tonight?

Sam immediately took off at a run after the fast-disappearing car. I hurried over to the house, where I saw that the side door was open. Not thinking of the danger, I stepped inside, turned on all the lights, and ran from room to room. Nothing seemed to be amiss. At a glance, everything looked to be in apple pie order.

Sam came running back home, dialing 911 on his cell phone as he went. We reported the break-in to the police, who came over to the house within record time to take our statement. What could we report exactly? It was all very mysterious. We thought that we saw at least two people in the getaway car as it sped away down our quiet street toward four-lane McIntosh Road and the Interstate. Quick-witted as usual, Sam had taken a photo of the license plate of the retreating vehicle as it careened around the corner onto the main road. The police could use that information as a start in their investigation.

When Jack and Jill, our experts on all matters criminal, got involved, they had a few suggestions for us to follow up on. I was surprised to learn that they had become quite involved with Waylan Cooper, of all people. It turned out that he and Jack had served in the same unit in the Persian Gulf. This created a bond between the two men, with Jack impelled to help his younger incarnation clean up his act. Waylan's bank manager girlfriend, Shelley Dupree, had been an excellent influence in heading his life in the right direction. She and Jack even had Waylan enrolled in school and hard at work, and it turned out that he had an aptitude and an appetite for both. Upon learning about the break-in, Jack suggested we talk to the neighbors to see if they had seen or heard anything that night.

We asked around, and our tenant in the coach house out back had seen a late-model Mercedes parked in the driveway for a half-hour or so earlier in the evening. He had assumed we had guests. He thought he had heard them out in the backyard for a while. *How had they gained entrance into the house?* Not even the neighbors' two pit bulls, Duke and Dukette, who barked at everyone, including Sam and me, sounded the alarm, silenced by two pounds of chopped beef that had been strategically offered by the culprits. We found telltale scraps of waxed paper meat trays from the *Publix* butcher department when we searched the neighbor's yard.

The police established that it had been easy to jimmy the side door lock. We immediately had more substantial locks installed on all the doors. As break-ins went, we had to consider ourselves lucky since nothing appeared to be taken. But what had been the motivation for the burglary in the first place, we wondered?

To my surprise, my neighbor on the other side of our house from the dog owners, Irma Maus, whose family was prosperous pig farmers originally from Minnesota, told me that there had been a string of break-ins in the neighborhood recently, which was most unusual. What was the world coming to, she wanted to know. Our neighborhood was solidly lower middle class and originally almost completely Mennonite. There was nothing worth stealing in the houses around us. The whole thing was inexplicable. Sam and I chalked it up to the random danger of modern life and got bids to install more outdoor lights around the perimeter of the property. Counting on the new light system and the beefed-up locks, I felt somewhat reassured. Ultimately, even the license plate number Sam provided to the police yielded no leads, so the matter remained unresolved for the time being.

———

Our next social engagement took place in one of the more upscale Sarasota neighborhoods, which was used to protecting itself from robberies with lights, alarm systems, gates, and security companies. Sam and I had been invited to attend Marybelle and Peter Thomson's holiday party at their gorgeous house on Siesta Key. Casually elegant was the attire of the evening. I wore black crepe palazzo pants and a printed silk top with a boat neck, against which my mother-of-pearl choker was shown off to great advantage. Sam looked dashing in his cream-colored linen pants and blue blazer.

Through their real estate business, Maresol, the Thomson power couple had really begun to transform the Siesta Key barrier island from a laid-back, feet-in-the-sand beach community to a desirable locale for the well-heeled. They had come up with an ingenious, soup-to-nuts sales approach, with Peter as the realtor and Marybelle as the interior designer. Their business plan could be tailored to suit the needs and desires of a discerning American and increasingly international clientele. Maresol Properties, LLC, would provide exactly the services required, from finding the oceanfront property, to designing and building the new construction, to placing the last artful gewgaw on the coffee table. These palaces, from sleek, low-lying, modern, glass and concrete styles to multi-storied Mediterranean villas with balconies overhanging the nearby waves like the prow of a ship, were also delivered fully landscaped.

I thought to myself that it was like a magic trick to watch how quickly a modest little 1950s beach house right on the water near Siesta Village could disappear in a day, leaving nothing more than a plot of sand, a view of the Gulf, and some sea grape bushes.

Next thing, a fence with "Maresol Properties" written on it would be erected to shield the emerging butterfly of a house from embarrassment during its ungainly chrysalis stages. The fence itself was good-looking, a stage set, completely blocking out the sand and sea, which created a mystery about what the view was like behind it. On the fence was painted an impressionistic rendering of the prospective house and discreet contact information. Everything about the Thomsons' sales approach and product was more sophisticated and stylish than their competition's heavy-handed, 'meat cleaver' sales pitch.

Marybelle and Peter Thomson's own home, where the party would take place, was fit to be featured on the pages of *Architectural Digest.* Marybelle had managed to take a rambling Sanderling ranch house and turn it into something spectacular. Yet I also detected traces of the comfortable family retreat I had noticed at committee meetings in the big den and open kitchen area. The house reflected both the owners' business acumen and their commitment to their family.

Sam and I were among the first guests to arrive, so I took the opportunity to show him around. I was pleased to recognize a couple of familiar faces in the crowd. Seeing Caterina Alvarez and a few other committee members I knew was comforting.

Caterina came over to wish us happy holidays. She took a moment to say that she had seen the photos Melanie had taken of the stone plaque at our house. She said she loved the pattern of the stone carving and expressed interest in coming by to see it.

A look passed between Sam and me. Here was another person who was attracted to our humble piece of stone. Before we could pursue this topic any further, we were separated from her by a swirl of happy partygoers. We were introduced to the mayor of Sarasota, a famous chef from downtown, and some people whose names matched faces featured in the city's glossy coffee table magazines. We also met the Thomsons' college-age son and daughter, who were attending the party.

At one point, Marybelle took me aside and, in her charming accent, asked how things were going. I thought she meant with my part of the committee work, lining up sponsors to provide refreshments for our foreign film party. She was, after all, the committee chairperson. In fact, she was interested in me personally, something that surprised and touched me. So I let my hair down and briefly filled her in on my unpleasant experience being locked in at The Ringling Museum. I told her that I thought that they owed me an apology for the insulting way their staff had treated me, accusing me of wrongdoing, instead of taking responsibility for their shortcomings.

Marybelle was shocked. "Honey!" she said, with that faint lilt in her voice. She was appalled to hear of my ordeal and asked if it would be alright if she looked into the matter on my behalf to see if anyone could be held accountable. It seemed that she had quite a bit of influence with the museum board members.

Needless to say, it was more than alright with me. It was very kind of her. I guessed this was what it was like to have influential friends in high places.

Sam and I wrapped up the season with a New Year's celebration with Jack and Jill and hundreds of other revelers downtown at the intersection of Pineapple and Lime Avenues, the very center of Sarasota, to watch the colorful, illuminated Pineapple drop at midnight in imitation of the ball in Times Square in New York. I was glad to see that Jack and Jill had buried the hatchet and were as happy together as two turtle doves for the moment.

Jack's investigations for ICE were promising to lead to paydirt. Always lots of promises, but no hard cash.

After the festivities, we went back to Sam's condo to toast to the new year and sing *Auld Lang Syne,* and eat canapés.

We turned on the TV to catch the New Year's ball drop celebrations around the world recap. The local Sarasota news came on afterwards, and we were surprised to hear a human interest story about The Ringling. It seemed this holiday season, someone had come up with a successful idea to raise a little money for the financially strapped organization. The scheme was called "Ring them Holiday Bells for The Ringling." The museum had sent out a mailing asking for donations at the sapphire, ruby, or diamond level. Depending on the amount of your donation, by return mail, the museum sent you a paper cigar band with a drawing of a red, blue, or white pretend gemstone. The campaign had really taken off. People from all around the country, especially from the upper Midwest and from Canada, had contributed to the campaign to support the museum. This campaign demonstrated that, beyond all expectations, The Ringling meant a good deal to people from Sarasota, from Florida, and to many snowbirds who visited Sarasota from all over the country and beyond.

"That was a clever fundraising idea. The holidays are always a good time to get folks to open their hearts and their wallets. Maybe there's some hope for The Ringling yet," Jack said.

"Here, here," Sam said. "Let's toast to a good year for The Ringling! And for all of us!"

Barbara wasn't feeling so warm and fuzzy toward The Ringling management at the moment, but underneath, she was pleased that other people recognized its importance as an irreplaceable cultural treasure.

CHAPTER TWELVE

"Go On, Take the Money and Run"
~ The Steve Miller Band

Like magic, right after New Year's, I received a call from the chairman of the board of The Ringling Museum apologizing for my experience at the hands of the security staff. He had looked into the matter and learned that I had indeed been left in the lurch by one of the security guards. I wondered if the speedy response had anything to do with Marybelle.

Director of Security Mc Bride had roundly chastised the errant young agent, who had been Employee of the Month not long ago, for the way he neglected his duty to me when he deserted me at the ladies' room. However, left unmentioned were my troubling assertions that no guards had been on duty nor alarms functioning the night of my sequestration and my unjust treatment at the hands of Security Director McBride himself. The board chairman asked if there was anything he could do to make me feel better about my bad experience with The Ringling security department. I decided to go for it, and I told him that I wanted the museum to do me a favor and hire a protégé of mine onto the security staff on a probationary basis. This deserving young man, an Army veteran in need of a second chance, could learn on the job and perhaps eventually be an asset to the security department.

I was, of course, thinking of Waylan Cooper and how he could be eyes and ears on the inside to find out what really happened the night of the security blackout.

The board chairman was surprised but did not dismiss my request outright. I reminded him of the City of Sarasota's program for rehabilitating veterans and provided Jack Gilbert's contact information, noting that Jack would know how to reach my deserving protégé, who qualified for the city's veteran assistance program.

Right after this call, very excited, I checked that Jack was home and hustled over to see him and Jill. I needed Jack to get in touch with Waylan to prepare him for The Ringling Museum chairman's offer.

When I arrived at the Gilbert house on Bee Ridge, who should I find lounging around the pool cage, looking cool in his boogie board shorts, but Waylan himself with one tanned arm around his bikini-clad girlfriend, Shelley. She was a delicate-looking, auburn-haired beauty, all peaches and cream, with long-lashed hazel green eyes. They made a striking couple, for she was as easy on the eyes in a feminine way as Waylan was an exemplar of male good looks.

Jack certainly kept his eyes trained on her. We all said hello to each other, and introductions were gotten out of the way where Shelley and I were concerned. Jill invited me to make myself comfortable in the circle of lounge chairs on the pool deck, where they were all seated. I studied Shelley for a moment. She was a more sophisticated kind of woman than I expected to meet in Waylan's company.

I didn't see any polite way to back out of there, so I put my legs up and leaned back in a deck chair. Maybe this impromptu meeting was for the best. I could present Waylan and Jack with The Ringling's job proposition and get their respective takes on it right away.

I knew that Jack had been in touch with Waylan and had taken a shine to him and Shelley. Jill had even done a 180-degree turn and become supportive of him. My friends were trying to set the young couple a good example to follow. Being role models seemed to bring out the best in them.

I launched right in. "You will never guess who called me today from The Ringling with a tentative offer of probationary employment on the security staff for none other than Waylan Cooper here, thanks to a few strings pulled by a well-placed friend of mine."

Jack said in his "you can't put one over on me" wisecracking style, "C'mon, Barbara. Get off your high horse. We were just talking about the slim pickings available on the job market for our buddy here, even though he has completed coursework in security management."

I assured them I wasn't joking around and explained all about my conversation with The Ringling board chairman. Their reactions to this news varied. Jill was delighted. She gave me a little hug and said she just knew the universe would make a position open up for Waylan and find someone to investigate my bad treatment at the museum. Waylan gave a hoot and a holler. He stood up and pumped his fist. He loved the idea of doing undercover surveillance work and getting paid for it. He already saw himself in uniform and in the hero's role.

Shelley was the stumbling block. She was adamantly against the idea.

"Waylan, this sounds dangerous. You could get seriously hurt," she simpered, taking hold of his arm. "According to what Jack and Jill have told us, something underhanded is going on in that security department. It's a mess. Maybe even those smugglers Jack is tracing for ICE are somehow tied into the museum."

"What are you talking about, Shelley?" I asked her. "Aren't you exaggerating?" Shelley was clearly no lightweight despite her delicate looks. I wanted to counter her negative influence on Waylan. I looked to Jack for support.

But I didn't get any. He told me about the latest Ringling-related developments he had uncovered. While investigating the mysterious telephone numbers that led from his Yemeni employees to the museum, he started looking into the museum's database, where he found puzzling inconsistencies and lapses in record-keeping from year to year. One year, an object was described and numbered in storage, and the next, it had disappeared or been renumbered. The museum's files and records were in such a state of disarray that keeping an accurate inventory of what the museum possessed in storage was next to impossible. The problem was particularly acute in the department of ancient Greek seals, small, highly decorative objects from the 1st to 3rd Centuries BC. The Ringling listed hundreds of them among their stores. Very few had ever been displayed.

"That's a fine kettle of fish," I said. "Do you think this has any terrorist connections, though?"

In answer to my question, Jack explained that he started looking at online auction sites and found a dead ringer for one of the ancient Greek seals from The Ringling for sale on eBay. And for a pretty penny, too. As an experiment, he placed a tempting bid, and before the item disappeared from the site, he was directed to one of the telephone numbers in Tampa connected to none other than Al Kader, the guy ICE was targeting as a terrorist suspect.

"What do you think of that?" Jill asked me. "You should see those Greek seals. They are beautiful. And I think the one Jack saw on eBay was a perfect match with the one owned by The Ringling Museum."

Jack continued. "It's a stretch, but think of this: as long as you are shipping out illegal cars, why not hide stolen antiquities in between the seats or in the tailpipes to sell at the destination on the black market. The Greek seals are easy to hide—small and beautiful. They look like gemstones. Very desirable to certain collectors around the world. But they are just an example. I think there is a ring of thieves emptying The Ringling storeroom of whatever is easy pickings."

Shelley spoke up, "And this is the kind of thing my boyfriend, Waylan, is going to be put in the middle of! It could be dangerous, don't you think?" The classy lady had an excellent point there. She was only trying to protect her man from harm.

"Hold on a minute there, baby cakes," Waylan told Shelley, removing her hand from his arm. "I appreciate your concern and all, really, I do, but you know I can take care of myself. This could be an opportunity for me. I know how to handle myself. I've met a few badasses out in the alley behind the bar."

"Shelley, I think he can handle that part of the assignment, if necessary," Jack replied. "But I'm counting more on his cunning and discretion."

Turning to Waylan, he admonished, "You must watch your back. Your front and your sides. But most of all, you must make everyone like you. Neither your coworkers nor The Ringling management must suspect what you are up to. You've got to seem like one of the guys—an ordinary trainee."

"Why, that's a role I was born to play—Waylan Cooper, good ole boy—right, Barbara?"

I had to agree that Waylan was mighty talented at seeming likeable and cooperative when he put his mind to it. He definitely fooled me into trusting him with my house and all its precious contents. Why, he had sweet-talked me into such a state of blindness, I would have sworn the angel boy could do no wrong.

Jack stressed the most important point of the assignment. "You must report your findings straight to me, no one else. Then we can get the police involved or get an ICE sting operation underway. By that time, you will be safely in the clear."

Shelley remained skeptical. She wanted to know if there would be any future benefit for Waylan in taking the risks he would be running. She was wise to think ahead, and of course, none of us could say where any of this might lead. At the very least, he might find himself permanently employed by The Ringling security department. If the ICE investigation really led to important arrests or deportations, the US government promised to reward its informants. But promises were easy to make and hard to pin down. The first step was to wait for the all-important telephone call from the board chairman's office, which would launch the reformed Waylan's career as a probationary security officer at The Ringling Museum.

Waylan's bravado overcame Shelley's reluctance.

I came away from our meeting kind of admiring his pluck. He resolved to accept The Ringling job assignment if it was offered.

———

With the holidays behind us, we invited Melanie and her beau over for a quiet meal at my house. Sam wanted to put the gas grill he had won at the company picnic to good use. It had found its permanent position in my backyard, where there was more room than over at his condo.

Sam was busy arranging things to his liking for the dinner. He was in his glory getting everything ready. On the menu was shrimp grilled in the shell, accompanied by a Sam speciality, blackened red and green peppers and onions, all done on the grill. Corn on the cob would be steamed in aluminum foil packets. A crusty loaf of French bread awaited in its basket in the middle of the dining room table. Sam's signature Bananas Foster flambé would cap off the feast.

Sam looked especially dashing in his jeans-style apron with leather trim. His muscular arms and capable hands were holding a brush and oil to apply to the spokes of the grill's grates in preparation for cooking. He was in his element. He loved food prep and serving. He even liked the clean-up. I was one lucky lady!

Vroom Vroom was unable to attend at the last minute; instead, Melanie was bringing Caterina Alvarez, the fashion designer she had met at the film festival meetings. They had been at their film festival luncheon event that very afternoon, right before our barbecue.

When they arrived, Melanie's attention was drawn to the greeting cards displayed on the mantle of the fireplace. She walked over to look at them more closely.

"Why, Aunt Barbara, you still have your Christmas cards up? Are they from Montpezat de Quercy?"

"Yes, I was waiting for you to see them before I took them down."

"This one is from my neighbor Héloïse, who asked

especially to be remembered to you, Melanie. She misses you at the Galax disco."

"How is she? And how's Déesse, her little dog?"

"Héloïse didn't mention her poodle, but she did say that her daughter, Colette, is doing well. She's in Toulouse, studying."

"The card next to hers is from our neighbor down the street, Monsieur Meunier. Remember him? He's keeping an eye on our house. After all, his specialty is keeping an eye out for things. He's a natural at that. He says that everything is fine at our place. No news is good news."

Melanie explained to Caterina how much she had enjoyed visiting Sam and me in the little French village where we spent the summer months.

"That is so nice!" Caterina exclaimed. "What an enriching experience for you. You know, changing the subject, I'd love to see that carved rock that you showed me in the photographs."

"Oh, I'd be happy to show it to you. I'll ask my aunt where it is."

"Yes, please, let's ask her about it. I really would like to see it."

At that moment, there was a rumbling noise outside in the circular driveway, followed by a knock on the door, which Melanie ran to open.

"Vroom Vroom! You've come after all!" she cried out happily.

"Yes, I was able to get away at the last minute, and I wanted to surprise you."

The way they looked at each other, I could see that the trip to Philadelphia must have gone very well. It had only made them fonder of one another.

We were delighted to include Vroom Vroom in our little gathering. I set another place at the table. Sam said there was no problem stretching the meal to include another guest. The delicious dinner was soon served, and we sat down to enjoy it.

Caterina and Melanie had a big announcement to make. The Sarasota Film Festival had a new sponsor, an Arab sheikh, no less, named Abdul Al Salah. The girls had learned about the new sponsor at the special film festival event they had attended that afternoon, which featured actress Alicia Silverstone, who was promoting her animal rescue efforts. It was exciting to meet her. She was very pretty in person. They had also met the sheikh, who had seemed very pleasant. In addition to the sponsorship, he had also made an extremely generous and very public donation to Ms. Silverstone's animal rescue compound. There would be a feature story with photographs of him presenting a big check to the actress in the newspaper tomorrow. A press photographer had been there to document it all.

Sheikh Al Salah had invited a few committee members to the US premiere of his own film, *Emperor Souleyman's Sultana,* which was one of the entries in the Sarasota Film Festival's Foreign Films category this year. Melanie and Caterina were among those chosen to receive tickets.

"Maybe you and Sam would like to come, Barbara? I think I could arrange it," Caterina said. "The committee has a few extra tickets to the screening. It will be one of the first showings at the Regal Cinemas on Main Street. As you know, the film screenings and the voting begin tomorrow."

"Oh, that's a great idea," Melanie chimed in enthusiastically. "Vroom Vroom is coming, Aunt Barbara," she said, squeezing his hand. "And by coincidence, the film is based on the life story of the lady whose portrait you saw painted by Titian in Paris, the one with the conical hat owned by The Ringling Museum."

"The concubine who became an empress? An Arab sheikh

movie producer sponsoring the film festival? Wow," I said, "of course we'll come. Right, Sam? You don't have to work overtime tomorrow?"

Sam said that he wouldn't miss the film. He loved the movies. We all started to help carry our plates into the kitchen. Sam shooed us away so he could get serious about loading the dishwasher.

As I was showing my guests to the door, I remembered something I wanted to ask my niece before I forgot. "Melanie, have you ever noticed that The Ringling has a small gallery devoted to the ancient art of the Arabian Peninsula? I wasn't even aware that there was much ancient art from that part of the world."

Melanie reflected for a moment. "Well, I know that John and Mable Ringling acquired a huge and assorted collection of objects when they were being deaccessioned by the Metropolitan Museum in New York in the 1920s. The Ringlings were omnivorous collectors. They bought hundreds of Ancient Greek vases and wax seals, Sumerian and Babylonian tablets, and Assyrian carvings, which were really outside of their primary focus, but John Ringling just couldn't resist what was probably a unique opportunity."

"Do you know anything about ancient art treasures from Arabia?" I asked Caterina.

"Oh, ladies, not at all," Melanie's friend demurred. "My field of expertise is fabric design and couture. I want to learn all about Arabian art for a new collection I am launching. That is why I would be so fascinated to see the rock carving that Melanie photographed with the inscription. Where is it? I can look at it myself. Won't you point it out to me, Barbara?" she asked.

"Gee, I'd be happy to, but this isn't the moment," I said, somewhat mystified by all the urgency. "It's serving an important function right now." I winked at Melanie. "Stop over some other time, and I'll give you a private viewing." My gaze wandered out the patio doors towards the gas grill.

"Well, sure, maybe you and I can check it out sometime," Melanie said placatingly to Caterina. "And we can all go to The Ringling's Arabia Gallery. Meanwhile, we'll see everyone tomorrow evening for the film at the Regal Cinemas."

"That's right. Of course. Thank you so much for a wonderful dinner and a lovely evening," Caterina said. "Goodbye, Sam," she called out to him.

"Thank you, Barbara," Melanie and Vroom Vroom echoed, and they were gone.

CHAPTER THIRTEEN

"MAY I HAVE THE ENVELOPE, PLEASE?"

The following evening, Sam, Melanie, Vroom Vroom, Caterina, and I were sitting in a row of seats midway up in one of the Regal Multiplex Movie theaters, along with a number of other moviegoers. Attendance was good. The showings of this year's foreign films at the Sarasota Film Festival had begun. Sam and I wanted to see as many as we could and vote on our favorites. The best foreign film would be chosen by the vote of the moviegoer, and the winner announced at the party that my committee was preparing. We were delighted to have free tickets to the showing of *The Emperor Souleyman's Sultana* thanks to Melanie and Caterina.

To introduce the film, Peter Thomson stepped out in front of the curtain in front of the screen on the proscenium with a dark-haired man of about forty years old dressed in an elegant white suit.

"Who is that exotic-looking man?" I asked.

"Isn't he handsome?" said Caterina.

"That's the sheikh," Melanie told me.

And indeed this was immediately confirmed when Peter Thomson addressed the audience with a warm smile on his lips, saying, "Ladies and Gentlemen, it is my pleasure to introduce you to His Highness Sheikh Abdul Al Salah, the producer of the film we are about to watch, which is his entry in the contest for this year's best foreign film."

Sheikh Al Salah bowed to Peter and then to the audience and said, "I not only have the honor to present my film tonight, which I hope will please you, but I am also pleased and honored to announce that I have become a co-sponsor of the Sarasota Film Festival to promote the great work that Peter Thomson and the Festival does to support the art of film..." There was light applause. He continued, "and to work to promote the many attractions of the beautiful city of Sarasota."

There was more sustained applause.

The well-spoken man then explained that his movie had a connection with Sarasota. "The heroine of my film was inspired by the subject of the Titian portrait in The Ringling Museum art collection. There is a legend that this European woman became a sultan's wife—a mixing of Eastern and Western cultures as far back as the time of Souleyman. I feel that true greatness for our cultures arises from both sources and not just one. We are inextricably linked. And now for my film."

The sheikh left the stage, and the curtain opened.

Sam said to Vroom Vroom, "Emperor Souleyman was a great warrior and had a huge army. I learned in school back in Romania that he conquered the part of the country near Hungary where I was born and made it part of the Ottoman Empire for four hundred years.

"Is that right?" said Vroom Vroom. "I bet there will be some battle scenes. I thought we might be in for one of those melodramas that Melanie loves."

"Vroom Vroom and Sam," I said, "I'm surprised at you two. I didn't think you guys liked the typical blood and guts, shoot'em up movies most men can't get enough of."

"Sorry to disappoint you, Barbara, but I love to see a lot of violence on the screen. It's so relaxing. Right, Sam?"

"Right, buddy, you said it."

That was men for you, I thought to myself, *at least when they spoke to one another.*

The lights dimmed. As the story unfolded, we saw red-haired Roxelana, nicknamed "Hürrem" (The Laughing One), win the heart of the fearsome sultan. She was Circassian, an ethnic group from the north Caucasus known for its beautiful women. She came to Souleyman's capital city, Constantinople, as booty captured somewhere on the vast plains of the Caspian steppe. As the irresistible Ottoman armies swept over everything in their path, Roxelana was taken prisoner and converted to Islam.

Back in Constantinople, the young Circassian slave was unmissable among the sultan's women with her red hair, hazel eyes, and light skin. But it was her light-hearted personality that entranced the emperor. Despite her lowly position sequestered in the harem under the thumb of the senior concubines and eunuchs, The Laughing One won the ruler's love with her beauty, intelligence, and good humor.

Gaining in power and assurance, Roxelana connived a way to lord it over the sultan's real family and first wife. She got Souleyman to free her and to marry her, something unheard of in the harem. When the sultan's son and heir from his first wife fell ill and died, it was his son with Roxelana who eventually became ruler after his father's death.

The movie held our attention. It had something for

everyone. There were lots of stirring battle scenes as Souleyman's armies advanced across the plains of Asia all the way to the gates of Vienna. The Turkish foot soldiers and mounted battalions were accompanied into battle by military bands, a novelty that roused their fighting spirit and dismayed their enemies. The besieging Ottoman forces only turned back from entering Europe because winter was approaching. They left the field voluntarily, unopposed.

The costumes and interior decor of the film were exquisite. The men all had beards and were dressed in embroidered silk caftans and conical hats. The women were dressed in western style, with low-cut dresses that were certainly not historically correct, but showed off their busty figures to good advantage. The long tresses of their hair, especially the red locks of The Laughing One, were left loose or pinned up in elaborate coiffures dripping with jeweled hair ornaments.

The jewels worn by both sexes were fabulously ornate. In the movie, Emperor Souleyman was depicted as a skilled jewelry maker whose creations featured enormous precious stones. He designed a gorgeous emerald ring for the beloved redhead who so beguiled him that never quit her finger.

The "Sultan of Sultans" was also a poet. He wrote poems to his sultana in the letters he sent to her when he was away on campaign. She replied by composing her own love couplets. When Hürrem fell ill and died, Souleyman was inconsolable. He built her a beautiful tomb like the Taj Mahal, just as Shah Jehan would later do for his beloved Mumtaz in India.

Souleyman lived for many years after Sultana Roxelana's death. At the conclusion of the film, there was a touching scene where he was buried at her side.

As the final credits rolled by on the screen, some of the poetic verses the lovers wrote to one another were recited in the background, translated with subtitles.

The lights in the theater went on. People headed for the door.

"Well, what did you think?" Melanie asked Vroom Vroom.

"It was OK," he answered. The film was well done, but the story was kind of predictable."

"How about you, Caterina? How did you like the movie?"

"Well, the costumes and sets were gorgeous," Caterina said. "Don't you agree, Barbara?"

"Yes," I responded. "I loved that ring the sultan made for Roxelana."

"And Sam, we haven't heard your opinion," Melanie asked, following Sam's retreating figure up the aisle.

As I expected, when Sam turned around to answer Melanie, he had a tear in his eye.

He said, "I loved the movie. It was so sad and so romantic."

Sam could be so soft-hearted and easily swept away by a good love story. It was one of the things I loved about him.

Over the next two weeks, Sam and I tried to see as many of the foreign film entries as we could squeeze in. On the night of the awards' ceremony, the courtyard of the multiplex cinemas, decorated with streamers and potted plants for the evening, was crowded with people, some of whom were wearing coats and even gloves as they held their glasses of icy wine, cans of beer, and soft drinks. Light conversation and laughter floated in the air.

Everything was going according to our committee's well-laid plans except for the exceptionally cool weather over which even Peter and Marybelle Thomson, the committee chairmen, had no control. There was a real nip in the air due to an unexpected cold snap. Sometimes tourists and even natives forget that when an Alberta clipper from Canada turned the weather up north really cold, Florida also felt the chill.

The cold weather added to the excitement of the evening.

The temperature in South Florida was usually mild by this time in February when spring weather typically arrived. But not tonight. The unseasonable chill gave everyone a chance to show off their winter finery from up north and wear something a little different—a change of pace from T-shirts and flip-flops.

I was wearing my leather coat with the fur-trimmed hood, which I had dug out of the back of the closet. My niece, Melanie, who was there with Vernon, had on a sweater and long pants instead of shorts. Caterina had on a beautiful pair of embroidered boots from her latest collection.

I asked Melanie how she thought things were going.

"It looks like all your committee work paid off," she said. "People seem to be enjoying themselves. You've got a good crowd despite the weather."

As she spoke, Peter Thomson came by carrying a load of soft drinks.

"Melanie and Barbara," he called. "Can you help me bring more cans of soda over to the bar, please?"

We were happy to comply. Peter and Marybelle had been very pleasant to work with, well-organized, good delegators, and also ready to pitch in themselves. Furthermore, through their connections in the community, the foreign film committee had arranged donations of food, drink, and paper goods from different sponsors to make tonight's event a success.

Just at that moment, my friends Jack and Jill came over to say hello. Their *entente cordiale* was still firmly in place, and they were getting along famously. They were some of the many guests who had bought a ticket to attend our event tonight and support us. Jack was eating a hamburger, which he put down on Jill's plate. He had overheard Peter Thomson's request.

"No need to carry those heavy cans, girls. Let me do it. Just show me where to go."

"Thanks!" Melanie and I said in unison, pointing him toward the storage area behind one of the long tables near the bar.

"Thanks for coming to be part of the festivities," I told Jill. "This is another friend of Melanie's and mine, Caterina Alvarez. I'm not sure you've met. She was on one of the committees with Melanie."

"Nice to meet you, Caterina," Jill said. "I like your boots. They must be from CAD, your boutique, which I've seen over on Saint Armands Circle."

Caterina nodded. Accustomed to compliments, she accepted this one gracefully.

"Glad to meet you, too, Jill. Barbara has mentioned you. So has Vernon, who's over there, next to Sam, grilling the burgers."

"Good for them. They're doing a great job," Jill said, smiling. "They're busy. What are you girls up to? May I help?"

Barbara explained that aside from mixing and mingling, she and Caterina were free until it was time for the announcement of the year's best foreign film. Everyone who had bought a ticket to a foreign film had been invited to vote for their favorite. The votes had been tabulated, and the winner would be announced at the end of the evening by our surprise attendee, a well-known movie star.

"Oops! Excuse me a minute, ladies," I said. "I see Summer Bogdanovich and her husband over there. They are friends of mine from Longboat Key. How nice of them to come! I'll just pop over and say hello to them. I'll only be a minute."

Caterina and Jill were left alone together. After a beat or two, Caterina asked Jill if she had had a chance to see any of the foreign films in the competition to win tonight.

Jill explained that she and Jack had seen a Scandinavian entry at the Burns Court Cinema.

"The film was quite slow-moving. We had a hard time staying put until the end. It was interesting, though, to see life in Stockholm portrayed as it was in the 19th century. There was a lot of snow!"

Caterina said, "I didn't see that one. I voted for the one I liked best. *Emperor Souleyman's Sultana* is its title. I hope it wins tonight."

"Oh, that's the movie about the real-life queen whose portrait is in The Ringling Museum?" Jill asked. "I liked that one, too."

Barbara returned to where her friends were standing.

"Here I am, ladies. You two don't seem to have missed me. And here's Jack."

"Yes, the supplies at the bar are all topped up," Jack told them.

Jill said to her husband, "That was nice of you to help out, honey. You know, we were talking about The Ringling Museum just now. Isn't it great that our boy, Waylan, is doing so well working over there?"

"Yes, indeed," Jack enthused. "He's working out even better than we hoped, Barbara. I need to fill you in about that later on."

"What's that all about?" Caterina asked, suddenly very curious. "Who is Waylan?"

I laughed. "Waylan Cooper is a young man who rented my house last summer. There was only one problem—he never paid me any rent. The only thing he left me besides a big mess was a stone carving with mysterious markings. Not exactly in keeping with the look of my Mexican hacienda. I never knew quite what to do with it."

"Oh, yes," Caterina interjected, "You promised to let me

have a good look at the carving, Barbara. You were going to invite Melanie and me over to see it."

"We'll have to get around to that soon," Barbara said off-handedly.

Jack continued, "Waylan's been through some hard times and made some bad decisions, but he wants to mend his ways. Some strings got pulled for him with The Ringling Museum security department and my friends at the police department. Wouldn't you know it, they hired him on probation as a security guard at the museum. He's doing real well there. They like him. It's like the fox watching over the chickens. With Waylan's checkered background, he knows just what to look out for."

Sam and Vernon finished cooking the hamburgers and came over to join our group.

"Hi, everybody," Sam said. "The food service is ramping down. It's almost time for the announcement of the people's choice for best foreign film. You girls are on deck," he said, meaning Caterina and me, who were in charge of getting people's attention for the big announcement to be made by Peter, Marybelle, and the mystery movie star.

I took off my jacket and put it on a chair as Caterina and I picked up the little bell ringers on a pole, which we were to use to quiet people down as we circulated through the crowd. Sarasotans were accustomed to this way of being called to attention. The same system was used at the opera and ballet to signal people that intermission was over and that they should return to their seats.

Peter and Marybelle were spotlighted at one end of the courtyard near a microphone set up by the ballot box. They made a handsome couple standing there. The big crowd eventually quieted down, and Peter introduced himself.

He explained how much he and Marybelle loved Sarasota,

where their real estate company, Maresol Properties, was committed to development with a difference—the intent to beautify and protect Sarasota and its cultural gems while attracting the right kind of investment to make the little city grow and prosper.

As I listened to his persuasive and skillful presentation, I thought to myself that Peter and Marybelle intended themselves to prosper first and foremost. But why carp? Self-promotion was what made the world go round.

Next, Peter introduced Marybelle. Her blonde tresses fell artfully around her pretty face as she asked everyone for a round of applause to thank all the sponsors and volunteers who had made the Sarasota Foreign Film Festival event a success.

When the clapping died down, Peter, dapper in his madras shirt with a sweater tied around his shoulders against the cool night air, addressed the crowd again.

"Ladies and Gentlemen. The moviegoers of Sarasota have an opportunity each year to vote for their favorite foreign movie screened at the film festival. The ballots have once again been tabulated, and I have the honor and pleasure to announce the name of this year's audience favorite."

With this, he took a small white envelope out of his shirt pocket and handed it to Marybelle.

"My dear," he said, "would you do us the honor and read out the winning entrant?"

Just then, a handsome, familiar-looking man came striding into the courtyard with enormous assurance. It was *Magnum P.I.*, Tom Selleck, himself, late of the hit show *Blue Bloods*. Everyone started to clap, and some people whistled. Tom was a local hero and had a big property right on the ocean on Casey Key, south of Midnight Pass waterway.

"Allow me to help you with that, my dear," Tom Selleck

said to Marybelle as he took the envelope she proffered. He tore it open, his eyes widening for dramatic effect, and he announced into the mic, "This year's foreign film favorite is *Mumbai Monster Mania*, a film from India, directed and produced by Dev Ray."

His pronunciation was flawless. The crowd clapped. A little clique of the film's supporters cheered loudly as a young Indian man dressed in an immaculate white tunic with a Nehru collar and many small buttons running down its front stepped forward to shake both Tom and Peter's hands before giving Marybelle a hug.

Tom Selleck quieted the audience down to listen to the Indian film director's acceptance speech.

Mr. Ray was very gracious. He praised his competitors' films and said he was especially pleased to win, given the excellence of the competition. He singled out *Emperor Souleyman's Sultana* and the Norwegian film, *Ellington,* for mention. He hoped that his movie's success in Sarasota would give it a chance at wider distribution.

Tom Selleck signaled for more applause and signed a few autographs as he conducted the winning director off stage and into the multiplex building, leaving us all a bit star-struck.

Melanie and I had rejoined our group of friends for the big announcement. Caterina was disappointed by the winner. She had been rooting for *Emperor Souleyman's Sultana* to win. Sam sympathized with her.

"I'm disappointed, too," he said. I thought the sheikh's film was very moving and well-done."

Vernon chimed in. "I didn't even see the winning film. Did you, Barbara?"

"No, I didn't," I admitted. "I didn't get tickets to that one. I don't necessarily like Bollywood movies, even if this one was atypical."

"Sam," I whispered to my boyfriend. "I'm tired. I'd like to go home now."

"Certainly, Barbara. That's alright with me. Will you excuse us?" he said to our little knot of friends. "Barbara and I are going to bow out now. I've got work tomorrow."

"Of course," Jill and Jack said. "We should be leaving soon ourselves."

Vernon put his index finger in the air to detain us for a moment. "Listen to this," he said. "Peter Thomson has just made another announcement. Dev Ray, the film producer whose film just won the award, is offering a trip for two to India sponsored by his film company. He's going to draw the winner's name from the ticket stubs. Did you write your names on your movie tickets?"

"Yes, we did," Barbara said. "But I'm not going to wait around for the drawing. I never win at raffles or the lottery."

"Oh, no, don't go yet," said Caterina. " You must stay a moment and hear the winner!"

"No way," Sam said. "I won a gas grill at my company picnic this winter. That about does it for me, I'm afraid. Good night, all."

Barbara and Sam headed for the exit when Barbara remembered something.

"Damn! I left my leather jacket on a chair near the refreshments. We have to go back and get it."

"Oh, Barbara, you didn't! It's a good thing you remembered before we got too far away. We'd better go back and look for it."

The two of us turned in our tracks and headed back into the courtyard toward the chairs where I had left my coat. As we approached the refreshment area, we were startled to hear a familiar name broadcast over the microphone.

Samuel Spitz! Will Mister Samuel Spitz please make himself known? Mister Spitz, please come to the microphone!

And that is how Sam won a trip for us to visit India and the Taj Mahal. And they say lightning never strikes twice! And it doesn't, of course, unless the lightning travels all the way from the Arabian desert. But we didn't know that then.

———

I was curious to hear how Waylan was doing at The Ringling, so I called Jack. I was surprised to hear that Waylan had been checking in with him by text every evening for the past month. The first texts were boring. Waylan made huge efforts to fit in with the rest of the staff and the security department program. At first, his 'provisional' status was made crystal clear to him at every turn. He was unwelcome. He didn't even receive a uniform. He was just being tolerated, and his only task was to tag along with the security guard with the pompadour as the young man went on his rounds.

The Ringling was a pink building. Waylan tried to be pink, think pink. He wanted to fit into his new environment, not stand out at all. He tried to befriend "pompadour" and some of the other guys on the security team.

The director, Elroy McBride, who had accused me of getting locked in the museum on purpose, never even deigned to acknowledge his existence or give him the time of day. His orders and directions were passed on to him through the other agents.

So Waylan's strategy was to make himself the consummate "inside" man. Waylan laughed when the other security officers laughed. He frowned when they frowned. Their concerns were his concerns; their little victories were his as well. He learned the galleries and their layout in the smallest detail, the slack times, and the more crowded hours.

To Jack's delight, after a month, one of the guards, a guy named Mike, stopped showing up for work, and Waylan was promoted to regular status. He was given a uniform and a locker in the employee locker room. This was a huge development, and Jack and Waylan exulted over his progress.

"That's great," I said to Jack. "I knew Waylan could do it."

The beige uniform, a symbol of Waylan's promotion, became his new workplace coloration. Once he was officially part of the team, Waylan tried to be everybody's buddy. He even became tolerated at lunch hour in the employee cafeteria and no longer had the "cooties." He could sit next to almost anyone. An employee named Zeb was the only holdout. Zeb was an odd duck who mostly kept to himself.

If the guys liked peanut butter and pickles, Waylan did too. In need of a loan of five dollars, don't mention it, ask Waylan. If they voted libertarian, guess what? Waylan did as well. Need a favor, no problemo, just ask you know who, good ol' Waylan.

Jack chuckled as he related Waylan's amazement at how easy it had been for him to make inroads. Didn't the others ever tire of such a spineless wimp in their midst? Evidently not. Only Zeb continued to keep his distance.

Waylan was happy to report that even Director McBride was not immune to his blitzkrieg charm campaign, and when he asked for the access codes to the off-limits areas of the lower-level storage areas and bay-side loading dock, the security director himself promised to take his request under consideration. He seemed impressed to learn that Waylan was taking night classes in security operations management at Manatee County Community College. In fact, Waylan had enrolled in classes and was working toward a degree in security management, having discovered a real vocation for the kind of work he was doing at the museum and seeing lots of potential for how its systems could be improved and modernized.

Eventually, even the lone holdout, Zeb, finally came around. Waylan was changing into his uniform when he noticed Zeb's locker door wasn't closed correctly. Trying to close it, he found it was blocked by a huge pair of shiny black diving fins, which he couldn't maneuver to make Zeb's door shut. Waylan took a chance. He carried one of the fins to his own locker and closed it in there. Now, both locker doors shut properly.

When he saw Zeb in the lunchroom, he told him, "Listen, I saw your locker door was left open, and so you don't get in trouble, I moved one of your fins that was blocking the door into my locker, where there was more room. I hope you're not angry."

"You did what?" Zeb asked, starting a slow burn.

"I didn't know you were a diver. I like snorkeling, too. I was just trying to help you out. You can have your fin back after work. You should keep them in the trunk of your car like I do."

Little by little, Waylan wormed his way into Zeb's good graces by leaning on their shared enthusiasm for boating, fishing, and snorkeling. One night when they were on duty together, Waylan was happy to look the other way while Zeb spent an hour down in the storage rooms beneath the galleries. "Sure, I'll cover for you, buddy," Waylan assured Zeb.

"What are you doing down there anyway? Can I help?"

Zeb told Waylan, "Just rattle your keys in this grate here to warn me if anybody is coming, you hear? That's what I need you to do."

"Does McBride know about your work in the storage area?" Waylan asked.

Zeb shot him a piercing look. "Yeah, it's copacetic. He

knows all about it. Don't you worry. It's the others I worry about."

"This is incredible!" Barbara gasped into the phone. "I knew there was something shady going on there and that McBride was in on it! That's why he shut me down so quickly when I said I had seen flashlights outside and heard a motor revving."

"Barbara, your intuition was spot on," Jack exclaimed.

"Wow, you'll have to keep me updated while Sam and I are in India. We are leaving next Monday while Sam's hydraulic valve plant is on a short break for machine maintenance. You've got WhatsApp, don't you?" Barbara asked her friend.

"You bet. Call me for an update whenever your busy schedule seeing the sights permits or if you need anything from those of us here on the home front," Jack said. "Have a great trip!"

CHAPTER FOURTEEN

Sam and I were psyched for the trip to India. It was quite a journey to get to New Delhi from Sarasota. We were flying from Miami with a stopover in Dubai. Since our hotels, tours, and meals would all be free in India, we had decided to treat ourselves to business class seats and had been able to snag a fantastic deal on Emirates Airlines. The flight time from Miami to Dubai was 14 hours, and then it would take another three hours to get to Delhi. Our travel time would span more than a day without counting the four-hour drive from Sarasota to Miami International across Alligator Alley, the four-lane highway that cuts across the center of Florida from west to east around Lake Okeechobee and through the Everglades.

Once at Miami International, we headed for the long-term

parking, mindful to tuck the parking ticket with our parking slot number into Sam's backpack so we could find our car easily when we returned home ten days later.

The overnight flight to Dubai turned out to be almost enjoyable. In business class seats, we could stretch out on the flat beds and get some real shuteye during the long trip. Emirates had an excellent reputation for in-flight service, and we congratulated ourselves again on our good fortune to have secured these particular tickets at such a low fare. Flight attendants in their smart beige suits and red hats with veils that stretched beneath their chins escorted us to an exclusive area of the plane that we'd walked through many times in the past on our way to our usual seats in economy. The experience felt unique and exotic.

This was living, we mused when a flight attendant offered us a choice of champagne or juice as we settled into our semi-private cubicles, complete with a designer flight bag of goodies, including an eye mask, earplugs, slippers, socks, hand cream, mini toothbrush, and toothpaste. There was even a spray bottle of scented water so we could keep our skin hydrated in the dry cabin air.

Sam was quick to test out our seats, adjusting his into the fully extended flat position for sleeping. Of course, I quickly followed suit, marveling at the ease and comfort. We perused the dinner menu as we sipped on champagne.

"We are fifth in line for departure," the pilot's disembodied voice said over the loudspeaker after introducing himself.

I noticed that his name and accent were British. Several of the young, good-looking staff were also Western. I'd read that a lot of occidental young people worked in Dubai and enjoyed the salaries and the lifestyle there.

Upon take-off, Sam and I were offered a selection of appetizers displayed on tiered trays and served to us on real

China set on crisp white linen tablecloths that covered our tray tables. The female flight attendants had removed their red veiled hats and now wore cute sandy colored aprons over their uniforms. It all seemed a little over the top to me, but Sam was enjoying the show, especially when the chef, donning a tall white toque, came around to inquire if everything was to our liking.

"Imagine what it's like in first class," he said to me. "Maybe the attendants put the food in your mouth for you like the maharajah's servants did for him," he joked.

I shot him a look. Sam was referring to a passage we had read in a novel about princely India, *The Far Pavilions,* in our attempt to learn something about India before our trip. We also read three other wonderful books, *Freedom at Midnight, Midnight's Children,* and *City of Joy.*

After the dinner and liqueurs were cleared away, I snuggled down in my bed beneath the cozy comforters and pillows that we'd been given. I was worn out from our days of preparation and the long drive across the state from Sarasota.

Comfortably ensconced on my cushioned pallet at 30,000 feet, I gave Sam a peck on the cheek and fell into a delicious slumber for several hours. Watching movies and enjoying breakfast and snacks alternated with periods where we dozed off. But at some point during the flight, Sam began to get restless from the forced inactivity, so we walked together to the galley area to do some stretches and forward bends. It wasn't long before the sun finally rose on the other side of the planet, and we were straightening up our seats and tray tables for landing in Dubai, where we would spend a few hours perusing the airport before boarding our connecting flight to Delhi.

Dubai is the world's busiest international airport and the hub for Emirates. I'd heard that it was designed like a big shopping mall in the United States. There was a massive and airy multi-level hall with a high ribbed ceiling lined with fast food eating places, casual clothing stores, and souvenir shops with pop music piped in from hidden speakers. The air conditioning kept us cool. We could have been in Chicago or Omaha instead of on the Arabian Peninsula.

There were a few differences, though—the men were dressed in ordinary Western clothes, but the women were completely covered, except for an opening in their headgear that exposed their eyes through a kind of mesh grill. Their manner of dress was very strange to me, and the grill over the eyes was kind of menacing. I noticed one woman in particular looking at me. She had the most beautiful, twinkling eyes. They were very large and deep brown, like agates. I could have sworn she was smiling at me under her veil because her eyes looked so friendly. The rest of her was completely anonymous, hidden under her burka.

Gold was for sale everywhere. The precious metal was on display out in the open on long tables covered with pristine white cloths. Spindles covered with gold chains of all dimensions, from skinny and delicate plaits to wide, woven bands, lined the tabletops. I noted that all the jewelry was the deep, rich color of 18 or 22 carat gold; merchants didn't bother with the 14-carat stuff we were more accustomed to seeing back home, and it was sold by the length and weight of the chain.

Fluttering around the tables heaped with bright yellow gold, the female shoppers looked like exotic birds shrouded from head to toe in sky blue robes, which billowed around them as they moved between the tables examining the rolls of gold chain. The intense blue color of their burkas and the sparkling gold color metal set off each other to perfection.

Why, we wondered, *would people want to stock up on gold*

chains like this at the airport? I left Sam mulling over this question and went to find the ladies' room.

The bathroom was crowded, and I was surprised to learn that some of the women were dressed in the latest designer fashions beneath their burkas. Mini skirts and crop tops were revealed at the sinks and in the stalls, but disappeared again in the blink of an eye as ladies adjusted their outfits and donned their burkas once more. It was like a magic trick. One minute, a modern woman was there, and then she was gone. Several women remained completely covered head to toe at all times.

While at the sink, I recognized the woman with the incredible eyes I had seen near the gold display tables. I smiled at her and tried to catch her attention. Flashing her eyes at me, she moved nearer. "Beware," I thought I heard her whisper under her breath before she turned and went out the door.

Did she just issue a warning? It happened so fast and was so unexpected. I shivered at the strangeness of it all. *I must have misunderstood,* I thought.

Departing from the ladies' room, I rejoined Sam, who was waiting for me by the water cooler.

"I've got some bad news and some good news," he said. "Our connecting flight to Delhi has been cancelled."

"Oh no! You're kidding," I moaned. "What's the good news?"

"Since the next flight is not leaving until tomorrow morning, Emirates is putting us up at a hotel for the night."

"Really? An airport hotel?"

"Yes, we're to meet at the information counter in fifteen minutes."

"What about our luggage?"

"They're bringing it so we can take it to the hotel. But we'll have to recheck it early tomorrow morning."

"Ooh! How early is the flight to New Delhi exactly?"

"Well, we have to be back here at 5:00 a.m. Dubai time is eight hours ahead of Florida time. The minibus will pick us up at 4:30 a.m. tomorrow, which will be 9:00 p.m. Eastern Standard Time for us on the previous day. That doesn't sound so bad. We hardly know what time zone we're in anyway."

Our luggage in hand, we waited outside on the curb at Arrivals for the transport arranged by the airline to take us to the hotel they were providing. The sun had set, but it was still so hot on the pavement that we could feel the heat through our shoes. Just as we were contemplating ducking back into the air-conditioned airport terminal, the minibus arrived to collect us.

We clambered aboard while our suitcases were stowed in the back. We were the only passengers, so there was plenty of room. As we drove off into the night, I told Sam that although it was a drag to have our flight to India postponed, I was looking forward to getting to see a bit of Dubai, at least through the window of the van. Sam heartily agreed with me that we might as well make the best of this delay. So far, most everything we had seen in Dubai was as familiar to us as our local shopping mall back home, except for the gold sellers and burka-clad women. The next thing we knew, despite our good intentions, we must have nodded off because we remember nothing of our ride to the hotel.

The van came to a halt. I couldn't have said how long we traveled, but I felt quite refreshed when I awoke with a start. The sliding door of the van was opened, and we got down and stood, rubbing our eyes. We were parked beneath a grove of tall, royal palm trees in a walled courtyard with a fountain in the middle. I could hear the soothing sound of ocean waves in the distance beneath the higher-pitched tinkle of the fountain as the jet of water fell in droplets into its marble basin. The elegant design of the basin reminded me of somewhere, and it came to me after a moment—the Piazza Navona in Rome.

Sam and I were ushered into the fanciest establishment I had ever seen, more like a palace than an airport hotel. Liveried attendants led us through the colonnaded entrance flanked by reflecting pools, one on each side of low steps, which we mounted, escorted by a bevy of uniformed employees who took charge of our luggage. Stepping through the elaborately sculpted portico, we entered a huge reception area where very modern sofas and tables sat in groupings on the marble floor. An attendant invited us to be seated on a low couch from which we had a sweeping view of the sapphire blue Arabian Sea on one side and a desert caravanserai on the other. I felt small and bedraggled in such a grand setting, but it sure was impressive.

"I'm not sure where we are," Sam said with a grin, "but somehow I don't think this is the Ramada Inn."

"No kidding, Toto," I whispered, not sure why I was speaking in a low tone. "We're not in Kansas anymore."

Another impressively dressed gentleman approached and offered us some refreshment. I realized that I was ravenous and I gratefully ate the pretty biscuits he presented, accompanied by little glasses of deliciously-spiced tea that he poured from an elaborate, silver samovar, making quite a ceremony of it.

"I am sure you would like to freshen up after your journey," the major domo said. "Won't you be so good as to follow me to your quarters, where you will find your suitcases, as well as everything you might need to make yourselves comfortable and at home in my prince's humble abode."

His prince? What was going on? I felt completely disoriented and out of place as I tugged at Sam's shirt sleeve, and thinking perhaps we should make a run for it. *But where would we go?*

"Wait a minute," Sam said to the butler. "This is all very nice, but where are we and what are we doing here?"

The butler smiled in a disarming and engaging way. "You are the most honored guests of my prince, Sheikh Abdul Al Salah. This is his palace on Palm Island, an artificial island he created in the Arabian Gulf, shaped like the fingers of a hand, the hand of God, Inshallah, As God wills.

"You met the prince in Sarasota at the film festival. He wants you, his honored guests, to feel entirely at ease here at his residence. He begs your indulgence. He will greet you himself shortly. Until then, he invites you to bathe and refresh yourselves. A meal awaits you by the swimming pool in your suite of rooms, where I will be taking you as soon as you desire."

"What about our flight?" I asked. "We're leaving in the morning for New Delhi. This is a lovely place and all, but how are we going to make our connection to India? I want to go back to the airport," I told the chief wazir, or whoever he was, in no uncertain terms. "Sam, what's going on?" I said to my partner.

Sam, who had caught on quicker than I, attempted to talk me down, "Barbara, you may as well sit down. I think things have been taken out of our hands. You said you wanted to see more of Dubai, and I think you are going to get your wish."

With a sinking heart, I accepted what seemed to be a *fait accompli*. We were the guests of—or perhaps detainees of—Sheikh Al Salah, the sheikh who made the film *The Emperor Souleyman's Sultana* that was shown at the Sarasota Film Festival. I was dumbfounded and thunderstruck. I had a flashback to the warning from the veiled woman in the airport bathroom. Was this what she was referring to?

As the prince's butler suggested, we followed him around

several corners and down many plush, carpeted corridors to the handsome double doors that led to our luxurious accommodation. In the tastefully-appointed sitting room, we found a delicious repast waiting for us. Figs, olives, and dates stuffed with blue Stilton cheese surrounded a mound of hummus dripping with tahini sauce. Of course, there were baskets of flour-dusted rounds of flatbread to scoop it all up. Skewers of grilled lamb and beef shashlik were arranged on a platter of rice pilaf studded with pine nuts.

Waiters stood by to serve us, but we demurred, opting to fill our own gold plates and sitting down at the low table in the corner to eat. As we enjoyed the feast, which also included honey-infused pastries for dessert, servants drew us a bath in the giant, granite soaking tub in the enormous bathroom, filling it with rose-scented water before discreetly withdrawing from the chambers. There were loose-fitting caftans and embroidered leather slippers left out for us on the big round bed in the center of the suite. At first, I refused to put mine on; I got as far as unzipping my suitcase to get out a change of clothes when I capitulated. What was the point of remaining in my wrinkled shorts? I slipped the beautiful caftan garment over my head. It was just easier.

Through a wall of windows just beyond our private patio was a small, private pool. To my surprise, a selection of burkinis had also been provided for us, so I asked Sam if he wanted to take a dip. It was so strange to feel so pampered and petrified at the same time.

"I don't know about you, Barbara, but I think I'll just relax here on these pillows," replied Sam, who was now comfortably positioned on the elegantly draped king bed. "I feel like a pasha of the Orient. And by the way, you look very fetching in that embroidered silk gown."

I was full of dread, but it was a relief to play along with Sam as if everything was OK. "Why this old thing?" I teased him. "I've had it forever."

Sitting down in the cushions next to him, we kissed tenderly. But I just couldn't let myself relax into the moment. "Sam, remember that woman who told me to beware in the ladies' room?"

"I remember," Sam said, looking troubled.

"Do you think her warning had something to do with Sheikh Al Salah?" My underlying fear resurfaced that no matter our present luxurious surroundings, our journey had taken an unexpected and unexplained detour. Kidnapped was another word that came to mind. "Sam, what are we doing here? Are we under some kind of house arrest?"

"I don't know, sweetie pie. I just don't know. I guess we'll have to wait and see what happens when Al Salah turns up."

"I hope he shows up soon to explain what we're doing here."

"Well, according to his butler, Al Salah won't make us wait too long," Sam said. "Here, try a piece of this delicious chocolate with the golden filling I found on the silver salver here. The notecard says that it's a specialty of Dubai." He handed me a little after-dinner bonbon.

Lulled by the delicious meal we had just devoured and feeling clean and refreshed after our soak in the big tub, there was nothing we could do about our predicament for the moment, so we tried to relax, leaning back on the fat bolsters arranged in the corner of this beautiful room. I almost nodded off.

Suddenly, there was a discreet knock on the vestibule doors.

"Come in," I replied.

Another server, one we had not seen before, entered the suite, wearing a more military-looking livery than the others, and asked us politely but firmly to follow him.

At that moment, my phone started singing in its tinny voice, "Start spreadin' the news. I'm leavin' today. I want to be a part of it—New York, New York," and I knew it was former New Yorker, Jack Gilbert, who was WhatsApping me. I had set his ringtone to Frank Sinatra.

Sam and I looked hard at one another. *Boy, did we want to talk to him!*

I was just about to answer the call when it went to voicemail.

"There is no time for that now," the escort with the military bearing intoned in a gruff voice that brooked no dissent.

He led us to another part of the palace, even grander than the areas we'd already seen. We passed niches set in the walls and passages hung with beautiful textiles on our way to a grand reception room. A fifty-tiered, two-ton crystal chandelier loomed over our heads, suspended from the coffered ceiling on a huge chain. Sheikh Al Salah greeted us with a bow. "Welcome, my friends, he said warmly."

Before we could ask him why he had brought us here, he silenced us with a finger to his lips. "All will be revealed," he assured us. "You have nothing to fear."

There was something about his commanding manner that compelled us to obey.

At that moment, his butler directed us to two delicate, gilded chairs in the first row of the ballroom, which had been set up with similar chairs arranged for a conference or performance.

We watched as Sheikh Al Salah, his robes undulating

around him with a swish, swish sound, paced back and forth, wearing a path in the lush, red pile of an enormous and magnificent Persian carpet. Back and forth, back and forth. His footsteps made no sound, but there was a manic urgency about his pacing. Sam and I shivered with tension and from the chill of the air conditioning. The cavernous space was preternaturally quiet, and then Al Salah began to speak.

"You must understand how alienated we in the Arab world feel. You must!" the sheikh pleaded and commanded at the same time.

We stared at him, fully at attention.

A vein throbbed in his forehead beneath his white headdress, and his dark eyes flashed. "With all our oil wealth, we Arabs are still viewed by you Westerners as head-rag-wearing, tribal hotheads, stuck in the Middle Ages." He spat the words at us, his handsome face contorted with anger and hurt.

What had happened to the charming, almost obsequious man from the film festival screening in Sarasota?

His glance dripped with disdain as he continued, "Even you," he said contemptuously, "nobodies who just happened to end up with my precious stone carving, look down on me—ME!, revered leader of an ancient race, richer than Croesus, a prince who could make you disappear from this earth with a snap of his fingers."

I sat frozen as he snapped his fingers under Sam's nose. He leaned so close to us that I could smell his cologne.

I swallowed hard and shrank back against the elaborate struts of my chair; Sam remained motionless beside me, his hands cautiously outstretched on his knees.

Stone carving? Is this what this was all about? The stone carving that Waylan left at my house?

Sheikh Al Salah suddenly seemed to forget about us and

was speechifying to the multitudes. He pulled himself up to his full height as he proclaimed, "I want to place myself and my people where we belong in the world's history. And I am in the process of doing just that by building a collection of my civilization's greatest treasures here—here in my desert kingdom—in the world's most beautiful, cutting-edge building designed by famed architect, Frank Gehry."

A moment of silence fell as he let that impressive name have its full effect on his audience. In this case, Sam and I.

I lowered my eyes as he continued with a flourish, "I will make the world's cultural institutions and their leaders accept my people's contributions to the progression of civilization's development." His powerful voice rose to a crescendo, half-prayer, half-exhortation.

The sheikh was carried away by emotion for a moment, then he suddenly returned to the present. Striding to the room's massive plate-glass window, draped with lovely silk furbelows, he beckoned us to follow him, which we did, scurrying after him like little robots.

"Look!" he bade us commandingly. "Behold my masterpiece of cultural redemption!"

We gazed out the window at an amazingly modern building totally faced with mirrored glass, brilliantly reflecting the white sand and desiccated bluffs of the desert landscape that stretched endlessly into the distance. It was an extraordinary sight, like a mirage made real.

"This is my museum," the sheik announced, staring transfixed for a moment at his creation.

His excitement was electric. Sam and I could almost taste his sense of pride and accomplishment. A servant suddenly appeared with three glasses of juice on a silver salver so that we could toast the daring and unusual museum building—the sheikh's vision, a work of art in itself.

I was impressed, I was awed, I was stupefied. How did this building get here in the middle of nowhere? Moreover, what could it possibly have to do with us? Apparently, it had something to do with Waylan's rock carving from back in Sarasota. More importantly, when would we be free to go? Why was the sheikh bothering with us?

I needed to get back to Jack's message. Perhaps it was linked to our current predicament. Last I remembered, we had agreed that I would call him for updates, but here he was calling me. But when would Sam and I have a moment to ourselves?

I was flabbergasted by the turn of events that had landed us tête to tête with a sheikh obsessed by world-class museum ambitions and the associated problems.

Sheikh Al Salah calmed down after his emotional outburst. The three of us sat down at the window together, looking out at the museum building and sipping our goblets of juice, which were refreshed by a liveried attendant.

I hazarded an exploratory remark with the aim of extricating ourselves from this crazy situation. "Sheikh Al Salah," I said, "the museum building is magnificent. The inside must be as stunning as the exterior. Would you consider showing it to Sam and me before we get on our way?"

"Certainly," the sheikh replied, his manner imperious and exquisitely polite at the same time. "That is part of the plan," he continued. "I want you to see where the inscribed stone in your possession fits into the place prepared for it—its rightful place." His dark eyes burned with excitement like hot coals.

Sam interjected, "The stone you reference, what stone is that exactly?"

"How can you two be so obtuse?" the prince upbraided us, exasperated with our naïveté, or was it cunning? "Where are you hiding the plaque with the ancient Greek inscription, which I know that you have in your possession? You taunted my informant about it when she tried to see it at your house.

She almost succeeded when you deflected her with some ruse. You boasted about its usefulness!"

My mind leapt immediately to Caterina Alvarez's curiosity about the hunk of stone that Waylan had bequeathed to me and her urgent desire to see it. I shot Sam a meaningful look, but he was looking at the sheikh, who announced, "I am prepared to negotiate with you. Come on now," he said in a wheedling tone. "How much do you want for the carving? Let's get down to business."

Sam replied, mystified, "I don't understand what you're talking about. We are not selling the stone."

The sheikh became angry. "Don't toy with me any longer," he threatened, "I need this carving. It is the lynchpin, the ancient Greek section of my Rosetta Stone, which will enable scholars to translate the Nabatean texts by working backwards from a language they know to decipher the Nabatean passage ... Enough!" he thundered. "You two are trying my patience! I had already negotiated a price with Al Kader before you stole the tablet from him."

"Stole?" I sputtered, looking at Sam in disbelief.

Al Salah went thundering on, "I have been patient, but I ..."

Suddenly, I was overcome with a malaise, a combination of fear, fatigue, and the unbearable tension of the precarious situation we were in. I could no longer control myself. I burst into tears and started shaking uncontrollably. "What are we doing here? Sam, Sam!" I cried. "I can't take it! I want to go! Please, release us!" I pleaded with Al Salah. "What can we do?" I collapsed in a heap at the sheikh's feet, sobbing and hyperventilating.

Sam knelt down to comfort me, but I wasn't in any condition to be soothed that easily.

I thought I was having a nervous breakdown. I thought I liked exotic locales and unusual experiences. I was interested in art and museums. But I also liked to be in control, and here I was clearly just a pawn on someone else's chessboard. We were supposed to be on our way to India. Instead, we were detained somewhere in the United Arab Emirates and unfairly accused of involvement in a crime. I couldn't handle it.

Sam told the sheikh, "We've got to do something for Barbara. She's unwell. If it's the stone tablet you're after, no problem. We'll do whatever it takes, but help her." I looked up at Al Salah and Sam, beseeching them.

In a flash, a more comfortable chair was brought for me. Smelling salts appeared at my side along with a glass of water, blankets, and a pillow. My feet were gently placed on a stool, and a gentleman with a fan stood by ready to give me some air. I immediately felt somewhat better and regained a little color. My breathing was more normal.

"Listen carefully, please," Sam said, addressing the sheikh. "We don't know anything about this. We didn't steal anything. We returned from our summer vacation in France and found the stone carving left behind at our house by Barbara's renter, Waylan."

"Wait a minute," I said to Sheikh Al Salah. "You were behind breaking into my house? That was criminal! How dare you! You would go to such lengths for a piece of rock!"

It was finally making sense. We thought it was simply a neighborhood break-in and that the car we saw fleeing our driveway was part of a local ring of thieves who had been targeting homes in our neighborhood.

Sam laughed derisively. "What a desperate move! We were not hiding the piece of stone. We had no idea that it was valuable, so I've been using it to stabilize the gas grill. I put it under the base to keep the appliance from wobbling on the broken tiles in Barbara's backyard. That's why your people couldn't find it. But you can certainly have it back. I can use a flat piece of wood or tile instead."

Our Arabian prince shook his head in wonderment. It was so simple the way Sam explained it. When the sheikh spoke again, he was shaking with relief and silent mirth. "I don't believe it," he said. "My coveted stone under your gas grill."

"Yup," replied Sam. "I won that grill in a raffle at work, and I just love it. It's better than the much smaller George Foreman grill I have over at my place."

Sheik Al Salah nodded thoughtfully, trying to imagine the object of his desire used for such a mundane purpose.

My heart rate returning to normal levels, I said, "Sheikh Al Salah, now that you understand that we did not steal the carving, it is safe and we don't want money for it, would you permit me to rest and regain my strength for a short time back in our quarters before we continue our meeting?"

I needed to get back to Jack to let him know about this incredible turn of events and to find out why he was calling me.

The sheikh had us escorted back to our accommodations. We agreed to meet again in the conference hall later that evening.

When we got back to our apartment, we sat down close together on the embroidered damask pouf, leaning against each other for a little support.

Sam said to me, "Do you think we're being shortsighted to refuse the payoff the sheikh offered us for the stone carving? It would probably be a big payday. Maybe we should consider it."

I got very quiet for a minute, chewing over his words, and then I asked, "And if we go rogue, what about the others who are involved, like Waylan, Jack, and Jill? Where does that leave them?"

Sam responded that Al Salah was so determined to have

the relic that he would certainly pay enough to share out among a few other co-conspirators.

I pointed out that the sheikh could be unscrupulous to get what he wanted and I didn't trust him. His minions broke into my house.

We each quietly thought about the variables of the situation.

I broke the silence first and said with an adamant toss of my head, "I don't want to be a co-conspirator!"

"Of course, you're right," Sam concurred. "I don't want to be one either—not my style. It would be a slippery slope getting involved in a plot to cheat The Ringling out of their property."

I gave Sam a quick hug, saying, "Let's stick to the straight and narrow path. It feels good to be humble and honest do-gooders. Let's contact Jack right away to see why he called and fill him in on developments. Why, back in Sarasota, they don't even know that we never made it to India!"

So I immediately called Jack and updated him and Jill on the unexpected and scary detour our trip to India had taken, which had all been a setup by Sheikh Al Salah. He was hellbent on getting hold of our piece of stone carving which was the missing part of a key which would help decipher the dead Nabatean language.

"Jack," Sam asked, getting on the line, "I have an urgent question. Where is the stone carving? Is it still underneath the leg of the gas grill over at Barbara's house?"

"No way, man! We moved it over here to my house yesterday to protect it. It's in my big, old-fashioned safe, wrapped in a baby blanket. It just fit. It turns out that stone is a valuable museum piece. Wait until you hear."

"Our boy, Waylan, has cracked The Ringling security department case wide open," he announced to us, his voice literally booming out of the little cell phone with pride and pleasure. In fact, here's Waylan, himself, to tell the story," Jack said. He put the handsome, young Floridian, as tanned as usual, on the phone's camera to recount the tale himself.

Sam and I settled back on the bolsters and pillows on our round bed to listen, feeling happy with our decision to stick to the higher moral ground. We had news of our own, but Jack was so excited, we let him go ahead. But first Jill insisted we use the camera to give her a little tour of our beautifully appointed room in the sheikh's palace. She oohed and aahed, and we waved to one another. Then Waylan got back in the frame and launched into a dramatic recounting of his recent activities. This is what he said.

"After a couple of weeks of befriending Zeb, my coworker in The Ringling security department who liked to snorkel, we were thick as thieves."

"Hey, Waylan," he asked me, "that outboard skiff you mentioned you owned? You want to make a little money on the side tomorrow night?"

"Whaddya got in mind, Zeb? How much are we talkin' about?" I said.

"Here's the plan. I'm on night duty here tomorrow night. You show up at The Ringling loading dock pier on the Bay at 3:00 a.m. sharp and cut your motor and your lights. No noise, you got me," Zeb instructed. "This operation is on the QT."

"Three in the morning? No lights? What are we up to? Are we stealing something outta here?" I asked him.

"And if we were? You got principles against making a killing for one night's work? Two hundred bucks, and bring your snorkel, mask, and fins. Also, a good underwater flashlight. We're going on a treasure hunt."

"That's what Zeb told me last week at work on Tuesday," Waylan recounted to his enrapt listeners: Jack and Jill, in their den at the house on Bee Ridge Road, and Sam and me in our suite in the sheikh's palace in Dubai.

"Go on, please," we begged.

"When I got to the back of The Ringling loading dock at 3:00 a.m. the following morning, Zeb was waiting for me with two burlap bags filled with lumpy, clanging, and heavy objects. We loaded them onto my boat, and Zeb directed me down the coast to Lido Beach, where we moored just off the sandbar. I immediately recognized it as my favorite yellowtail grouper fishing hole."

"Cut the motor," Zeb ordered.

"What are we waiting for?" I asked.

"We'll get a signal when it's safe to head into the dock. Meanwhile, let's get on our suits and snorkels and start checking around here for something that might have dropped on one of my last trips."

"You mean you've done this before?" I asked Zeb. "What kind of operation have you got going on? You're taking stuff from The Ringling storage and selling it? Is Director McBride in on it, too?"

Zeb said, "McBride gets his cut. He collects these little Greek seal things, like gemstones; there are hundreds of 'em in The Ringling storage. I think he sells them. Anyway, he keeps his mouth shut. You get in the water and look around for an object we might have dropped."

"A gemstone? Are you crazy? How am I gonna find something like that?" I asked.

"No, a rock, a carving with writing on it. Here, take this flashlight. There's big money in it for the one who can find that carving," Zeb informed me.

"That's when I realized it was deja vu all over again, as Casey Stengel once said." Waylan paused for dramatic effect. "I had already found the carving Zeb was talking about the day I hit my toe on it near the sandbar. Still, I had no choice but to go through the motions of searching the ocean bottom for something I knew was high and dry at Barbara's Spanish-style hacienda—because I had left it there myself!

"After I pretended to search for an hour, me and Zeb hauled ourselves back onto the skiff, dried off, dressed, and waited for a signal from shore. When Zeb spotted the blinking light he was expecting, we headed to a small dock behind a business premises on Saint Armands Key, where a man was waiting to take the heavily laden burlap bags off our hands.

"Where are we?" I whispered to Zeb.

"Enough of your questions!" Zeb hissed at me. "What do you care? Some fancy dress shop." I saw a box marked *CAD,* which I made a mental note of. I thought it might stand for CAD CAM, like in Computer Aided Design. I told Jack about it."

"Did you find it?" a thin man with a heavy Middle Eastern accent asked us.

Zeb looked at the guy and gestured with his open hands to show that our underwater search had come up empty.

"How could you have lost it?" the thin man yelled. "Al Kader wanted me to rough you up good for that." He shook his fist at Zeb. "Get out! You're finished," he said, "This whole setup is finished. Idiot! That stone was our ticket to the big money. The other items dwindle in importance by comparison. Here's your money," he said, pressing a wad of bills into Zeb's hand. "We are closing down this racket. The ICE people are onto us. Disappear back into the swamp you crawled out of!"

He picked up the bags of loot, left the premises, and drove off into the early morning in a late model Jag.

"What now, Zeb?" I asked my accomplice. "Where's my cut?" Zeb gave me the promised $200. "That's it for my trouble?" I said. "You need me to take you back up the coast to the museum in addition?" And I took him back up to The

Ringling to pick up his car before hurrying on over to Jack's with the recording."

"What recording?" Sam and I asked?

"I recorded it all on my phone," Waylan told gleefully.

Now that was the cheeky, daring Waylan Cooper I knew and loved!

CHAPTER FIFTEEN

"From the Desert's Heart, A Kingdom Arose …"
~ Song of the Nabateans, Christina Nova

The desert winds were dying down, and the sun was sinking into the Persian Gulf. It was the golden hour, as they called the time right before sunset here in Dubai. Sam and I retraced our steps along the carpeted hallway to our evening rendezvous with Sheikh Al Salah back at the grand ballroom, escorted as usual by a royal attendant. As soon as we were ushered into the sheikh's presence once again, Sam and I sensed a softening in his attitude toward us. He seemed less disdainful and more accommodating. I appreciated this friendlier approach and hoped it lasted.

Sheikh Al Salah intoned, "Come," in that way they have in the East that is both a command and a warm invitation at once.

A waiting butler, responsive to his master's whims and desires, immediately preceded us to some doors hidden behind the draperies, which he flung open. We stepped out into a portico where the largest white SUV I had ever seen—and I'm including Miami Beach and south Florida—was parked, waiting.

We all piled into the car. Fearful, I asked where we were going, and before I got an answer, we were whisked across the sands to the nearby glass-covered museum building and helped to alight at the entrance.

"You wished to tour my museum. I shall escort you around personally," the sheikh said. "I want to show you why the stone you have in your possession is so important to me and to my museum."

The edifice was drop-dead impressive. Sheikh Al Salah explained to us that every security measure known to technology had been installed to protect his museum collection, including elaborate climate control equipment.

The sheikh led us into the gallery, rigged out like the interior of the Parthenon, if the Parthenon hadn't been destroyed by the Venetians in the 17th century. We entered the sanctum sanctorum, deeply impressed by both the purity of the design of this temple and combination of tented space. It was breathtaking.

"You know many Arab people, my people, are not interested in exploring and excavating archaeological objects from the Arabian Peninsula from before Muhammad's time," the sheikh explained. "They fear that this will distract people from the purity of our religious ideas. I, on the other hand, do not feel like that at all. I think that it is important that we, the Arab people, demonstrate our solidarity with the great movement of cultural growth that has led to humankind's advancement from ancient times until today. That is how we will gain respect from the West, by showing we are an integral part of that cultural movement.

"The Nabatean civilization that arose in Arabia in ancient times played a part in the advance of science and learning and has been unjustly forgotten," he railed. "They built the city of Petra, as the Romans called it, and its magnificent Treasury, which you may have heard of. Their famous southern capital city was called Hegra. Its temples, tombs, and monuments were carved out of red stone. The Nabatean civilization made significant contributions to the Greeks and the Romans, who succeeded them, and I want to show that we all have a common background. To that end, I have put together a collection of carvings that illustrate the Nabateans' greatness and importance.

"I want to rescue the Arabian people from the backwater of cultural history and place their contributions in the mainstream of cultural progress. That is why I am so excited to assemble these ancient carvings and inscriptions, which show the Nabatean people's rightful place in the forefront of developments at that pivotal time in early history.

"This is my collection," the sheikh announced dramatically, as a curtain withdrew and revealed the objects he had painstakingly assembled at great trouble and expense.

I was impressed. I was awed. I snuck a look at Sam, who was enrapt like me, studying the sheikh's beautifully illuminated and displayed collection of sculptures and carvings. Around the peristyle of the room, he had assembled a sort of Elgin marbles in Arabian style, showing every aspect of the considerable accomplishments of a lost civilization. Under each primitive but powerfully rendered sculptural composition, there was an inscription that was inscrutable to us. Discreet placards set at a comfortable reading level beneath each assemblage were ready to translate the ancient inscriptions on the panels above us.

The sheikh continued, "You will note that many of the

explanatory placards are empty, waiting to be filled in. There is a reason for this omission. The ancient Nabatean language has not yet been translated. As it was at one time for hieroglyphics, the Nabatean language is presently a mystery.

"But just as Champollion deciphered the Rosetta Stone of Egypt, when I have the missing piece of stone tablet, we can start to break the code of the Nabatean language."

Al Salah shone a light on a stone carving that resembled the one at our house in both color and general appearance. As we inspected it, we saw two short paragraphs, one on top of the other. The markings of the writing in each paragraph were in different scripts, one on top of the other. The bottom of the stone was ragged as if it had been broken off.

The sheikh said, "The third inscription got separated from the first two. It is the stone carving in your possession that completes the key to deciphering ancient Nabatean. Starting from the ancient Greek sentences on your carving which experts can read, they can work backwards through the intermediary passage in an ancient Arabic tongue to get clues to revealing the alphabet of the Nabatean section. That is why the tablet in your possession is so precious to me. I must have it to unlock the secrets of this lost world of ancient Arabia, which I have rescued from the sands."

"What does the writing on your Rosetta Stone and our stone carving mean?" Sam asked the sheikh.

"The answer to that question is very interesting. The Nabateans had perfected a system for finding and channeling water in their desert kingdom, an invention that was new to the Greeks," Al Salah said. "The inscription is a formula that explains in part how they accomplished this technological marvel in such desertic conditions. The important thing is that it says the same thing in the three languages—Greek, an ancient form of Arabic, and Nabatean—so that experts can use it to eventually unravel the rest of the Nabatean alphabet from the letters they identify from the other languages on the tablet. It is also very significant that King Ptolemy V and his reign are mentioned because the name 'Ptolemy' is a starting point in all three languages."

He instructed us to look up at the clerestory of the temple structure where we sat. "Do you see the carvings around the peristyle?" he asked.

We looked up and saw the decorations he meant. "Look at the missing space in the middle there. That is where my inscription, the stone carving you put under your gas grill, belongs. The stone carving and the series of Nabatean writings it translates prove incontestably that the groundbreaking advances of Greek art and philosophy grew out of advances and developments here on the Arabian Peninsula. In other words, a contributing source of Greek and, therefore, Roman civilization—Western civilization—was dependent on discoveries and breakthroughs made by my ancestors, here, here in the Middle East.

"I want that stone carving. I need it as the centerpiece of my demonstration that my country and my people contributed to world culture."

Sam and I gave one another a meaningful look, finally understanding our role in this intrigue.

I spoke up first. "Sheikh Al Salah, we are not after money. We are not holding you up for ransom over the rock carving. We had no idea what it was. We have it in our possession completely by chance. We just learned tonight that it had been mistakenly dropped into Sarasota Bay by the thieves who pilfered it from the storage vaults of The Ringling Museum. They were taking all kinds of things, taking advantage of the museum's poor record keeping and a security director who was turning a blind eye to their activities as long as they cut him in."

Sam cleared his throat cautiously and asked, "Did you put in a custom order for them to steal the stone carving for you because you had researched it and found out from your sources that it was at The Ringling? I have read that some unscrupulous collectors do this kind of thing when they are determined to have an item for their collection."

Sheikh Al Salah exploded, "Where did you get this idea? Who told you that! You are really offending me," he vituperated. "No, not at all, the carving was proposed to me on the internet by an intermediary. Maybe that person did research and knew it was at The Ringling and that I would buy it for a high price if they could get hold of it. It is well-known in the art world that my representatives are always on the lookout for Arabian antiquities and that I will pay big money to acquire what I am interested in."

I hesitated a little to deliver my message. "Well, then, you will now understand that the carving you are so anxious to acquire is not our property to dispose of. It rightfully belongs to The Ringling Museum. If we give it to you, we will all be committing a crime."

Silence reigned.

The sheikh seemed so offended by the slightest imputation that he might have been willing to go to any means—even shady ones—to get hold of the missing piece of the Arabian Rosetta Stone, that I was taken aback for a moment. Then I wondered if he wasn't overdoing it. It seemed a case of "he who protests too much." I mean, he was behind breaking into my house!

I looked at Sam meaningfully, and he held my gaze for a moment and shrugged. Perhaps he was thinking along the same lines.

I soldiered on. "I heard you speak when you were showing your film, *Emperor Souleyman's Sultana* at the film festival, which we really liked by the way. You seemed genuinely interested in becoming part of the Sarasota community. Perhaps there is some way you and The Ringling Museum can cooperate, so that you can display the carving in your collection on permanent loan or something, and this phenomenal collection of yours can be an adjunct part of the museum."

After this, none of us quite knew what to say. We were all flabbergasted—completely surprised at the way things had turned out.

Then I had a suggestion, which broke the spell. "You know, Sheikh, I was really hoping to see a little of Dubai as long as we are here. It would kind of make up for the trip to India, which we thought we had won and seems to have been a desert mirage."

Al Salah scratched the little beard on his chin thoughtfully and then smiled at me.

"It is only right," he intoned. "That will give us all time to consider how to resolve this delicate situation in the most satisfactory way."

He clapped his hands. The SUV driver and attendants appeared again, and we were on our way to Palm Jumeirah, the fanciest, ritziest part of Dubai. From there, we headed to see the world's tallest building, the Burj Khalifa. And after that, a sumptuous dinner in an elegant restaurant.

During our few days touring around Dubai, we learned that the UAE is made up of seven emirates, with Abu Dhabi as the capital. The country is at the eastern end of the Arabian Peninsula between Oman and Qatar, with a long coastline on the Persian Gulf. Its population is 10 million, of which eleven percent are native Emiratis.

Dubai is the most populous city, and we enjoyed our time there. The official language is Arabic, the official religion is Islam, but the most spoken language is English, which is also the language of business. In the 21st century, the economy has become less reliant on the country's considerable oil and gas reserves and more on tourism and business. Sam and I were amazed at the number of shopping malls.

It was good to know that, thanks to Sheikh Al Salah, there would soon be a world-class museum to display artifacts that would no doubt be unearthed from the sands—evidence, he contended, of his civilization's significant contribution to the development of world culture.

After another day in Dubai, Sam and I flew back to Miami courtesy of Sheikh Al Salah and returned to Sarasota. The sheikh followed in due course on his own, in his private jet. Our little posse of Melanie, Vroom Vroom, Jack, Jill, Waylan, and Shelley greeted us enthusiastically and gave us a hero's welcome. Basically, our favorite, a big barbecue.

We were surprised to find a blitz of media coverage in full swing, featuring the federal investigation by ICE authorities of prominent Tampa Bay businessman Mohammed Al Kader for suspicion of financing terrorist activity, grand larceny auto, and theft of antiquities. Also detained and being held for questioning were his purported associates, a band of Yemeni nationals living modestly in Sarasota, doing odd jobs by day and stealing at night.

The public was especially riveted by Ringling security guard Waylan Cooper's TV interview in which he explained how, many months before the ICE investigation, he had innocently stumbled on a stone artifact the thieves had dropped overboard in the water off Lido Key. He had thought it might have some curiosity value, but never guessed that it was a one-of-a-kind stone inscription, the key to unlocking an ancient language.

But what about the present whereabouts of the stone plaque, which the sheikh coveted so much but which was the property of The Ringling? It was returned to its rightful owner —The Ringling Museum—now completely cognizant of the great treasure it possessed.

EPILOGUE

I n the next year, the declining fortunes of The Ringling
were completely turned around. Impressed by the
outpouring of support for the institution demonstrated
by the city of Sarasota's "Ring them Holiday Bells for The
Ringling" fundraiser, which raised over $50,000 for the
institution, the State of Florida handed responsibility for the
management and finances of The Ringling Museum and
property over to the University of Florida system, transforming
its possibilities.

Eventually, a new museum entrance, ticket sales area, gift
shop, and Italian restaurant were constructed. The Asolo
Theater was moved, renovated, and restored along with
Mable's Rose Garden and the Cà d'Zan mansion. The
Ringling's entire physical plant—the galleries, courtyard,
porticos, balconies, as well as the behind-the-scenes areas of
the museum—was upgraded and repaired.

An individual supporter gave a huge donation to build a
new circus museum on the grounds to house his collection.

Of most interest to our story, the newly elected museum

trustees entered into an agreement with a private collector, Sheikh Abdul Al Salah, to partner with his History and Heritage Museum in Dubai, called *Mather-Al-Athar* in Arabic. It featured an incredible collection of Arabian antiquities, the jewels being the two middle sections, which, along with The Ringling's stone plaque, completed the Rosetta Stone of the Nabatean language.

An elegant soirée took place on the opening night of the joint exhibition of Arabian artworks possessed by the two cultural bastions, The Ringling Museum in Sarasota and the History and Heritage Museum in Dubai. It was attended by all the glitterati of southwest Florida and many eminent representatives from the United Arab Emirates. The event and the exhibition attracted a lot of press attention in Florida and in wider social and cultural circles, as well as internationally.

The sheikh took the opportunity of the gala to announce his intention to finance a new gallery at The Ringling to house their future collaboration—a joint Arabian collection that would rotate between Dubai and Florida. Such a close partnership with an Arab prince was considered daring and controversial in some quarters. It really put Sarasota and The Ringling Museum on the map in this new field of artistic study.

Sam and I were unable to attend the event as we were traveling on an all-expense-paid tour of India's golden triangle of Delhi, Benares (Varanasi), and the Taj Mahal, offered to us by Sheikh Abdul Al Salah in recognition of our contribution to fostering international cooperation in the arts.

My niece, Melanie Renaldi, represented us at the gala evening. Her picture, along with that of her escort, Mr. Vernon "Vroom Vroom" Verdon, appeared in the Style section of the *Sarasota Tribune* along with those of other fashionable, younger attendees at the event, such as newly-appointed

Security Director Waylan Cooper and his accompanying person, Ms. Shelley Dupree.

ICE, United States Immigration and Customs Enforcement, never did come through with any reward money for Jack Gilbert, but they did charge and arrest Al Kader and the people involved with him in the terrorist smuggling ring in Tampa and Sarasota. ICE said that Jack's information had not led directly to the arrests, so he was not entitled to a monetary reward.

While Jack and Jill did not receive the ICE reward money, their company, Jack and Jill Gilbert Tile Company, was engaged to design and install the special flooring, which will enhance the new additions to The Ringling Museum. Their company will also refurbish all the museum's original tile and terrazzo floors, so in the end, their investigative work paid a dividend.

Under investigation and missing from Sarasota was Caterina Alvarez, of Caterina Alvarez Designs (CAD), whose boutique on St. Armands Circle has been shuttered for many months. It is rumored that the property is encumbered with a year of unpaid taxes.

Ex-Ringling Museum Security Director Elroy McBride and his accomplice, Zebulon Pike, were fugitives and were reported wanted by the authorities.

Jack Gilbert recently passed on to me a report that airline passengers E. Stavros McPapadapoulos and Zacharias Pappas arrived in Greece with one very heavy suitcase between them. They were checking into a fancy boutique hotel on the island of Mykonos when Interpol identified them as the missing suspects from Sarasota and detained them for possession of stolen Greek antiquities.

AFTERWORD

Back in France for another summer at our house in Montpezat de Quercy, I picked up the schedule of films showing at the local movie theatre in Caussade for the coming month.

"Sam, look at this," I said. "They're showing *Emperor Souleyman's Sultana* at the cinema in Caussade next Tuesday and Saturday. They've got the French and the original version."

"Yeah? Small world," Sam said, peeking over my shoulder at the fold-out schedule. "Let's give that one a pass. We already know the story."

I smiled, in complete agreement.

THE END

Lost, An Ancient Artifact Adrift in Sarasota Bay, is the th
art-related mystery where two well-intentioned American travel
unexpectedly become involved in an ICE investigation, a terror
financing scheme, and insider art museum dealings. Can t
unwitting couple help save an important cultural object
posterity—and shed new light on the Middle-East's little-kno
contribution to the development of Western civilization?

*Winner Runner-up Best Sequel
Hollywood Book Festival 2025*

*A 2025 New York City Big Book Awar
Distinguished Favorite*

*Kirkus Reviews: "An often fun and
fast-paced mystery…"*